J. H. Ward

Ballads of Life

J. H. Ward

Ballads of Life

ISBN/EAN: 9783744786768

Printed in Europe, USA, Canada, Australia, Japan

Cover: Foto ©Andreas Hilbeck / pixelio.de

More available books at **www.hansebooks.com**

Yours for the "Right"

J. H. Ward.

BALLADS OF LIFE.

BY

J. H. WARD,

Author of "The Hand of Providence," "Gospel Philosophy," etc.

ILLUSTRATED WITH NUMEROUS ENGRAVINGS, FROM ORIGINAL DESIGNS DRAWN BY WEGGELAND.

WRITE to the mind and heart, and let the ear
Glean after what it can. The voice of good,
Or graceful thoughts, is sweeter far than all
Word music; and good thoughts, like great deeds, need
No trumpet.

SALT LAKE CITY, UTAH:
JOS. HYRUM PARRY & Co., PUBLISHERS.
1886.

To THE YOUNG,

In the Commencement of Life's Journey:

To THE MIDDLE-AGED,

Surrounded by Cares and Conflicts:

To THE AGED,

Who have Toiled and Suffered:

To MY EARNEST FRIENDS EVERYWHERE:

This Little Volume is Inscribed

BY THE AUTHOR.

CONTENTS.

CONTENTS.   iii

PAGE.

My Native Land,   125
Children at their Play,   .   127
We've Drunk from the Same Canteen,   128
Who Was He?   .   .   129
The Mountain Boy,   . 133
Toward Sunset,   .   134
The Bachelor's Confession,   . 135
The Land of Rest,   .   138
Eternity,   .   . 139
Earth's Tribute,   140
Hold Still, ... 141
Comforting Words to those who have Lost their Children, 143
Fidelity and Honesty,   .   .   . 145
A Legend of the Maelstrom,   147
Mignon, ... 157
The Castle of Boncourt,   159
The Indian's Revenge,   . 162
Wynona,   .   .   168
Hero and Leander,   .   . 180
Hope,   .   187
Judas,   . 189
Change, .   .   .   193
Past and Future: A New Year's Rhyme,   . 195
To Unseen Friends, .   .   197
Requiem to Gen. Grant, .   . 198
Unknown Heroes,   .   200
A Noad to Blondin,   . 201

ILLUSTRATIONS.

PREFACE.

WHAT ! challenge the public to read your thoughts? Yet that
is really what an author does when he writes a book.

I know, alas, too well, that many of my thoughts are not
worth a memory; but, perhaps, my best thoughts, clothed in my
best words, and these, culled and selected during twenty-six
years, may be worth a momentary glance. Some of these pieces
have been published and republished. At first my name was
attached to them; then other papers copied them, and to them
appended the word "Selected." Some of them have been republished in books, with the easily-spelled word "Anon." placed at
the bottom, or even assigned to some other author. It is my duty
to acknowledge my poetical children, and a pleasure also, seeing
they have made themselves useful in the world of letters.

These "Ballads" have been written under varied circum-
stances,—in the old-fashioned farm-house, in the bustling railroad
depot, on the broad and lonely prairie, in far northern wilds,
mid the children of the forest, and some even in a soldier's tent,
with a drum-head for a writing desk, while watching at the bed-
side of a wounded comrade.

The "Translations" are from various authors—Chamisso,
Louis, Frichette, Goethe, Reinick, Schiller, Seume Uhland, Rittermann and Julius Sturm. In some instances bungling translations
of these authors are in print. In such cases the original text and

a more correct translation has been placed on opposite pages, so
that the critical reader may compare them.

To use the words of another, "Here, wrapped up in words, lie
those thoughts that floated through the brain, and those feelings
that burned in the heart, and were the hidden motives of outward
action."

The critic will, no doubt, see in these compositions many a
faulty rhyme,—many a sentence which might be improved. We
may comfort ourselves, however, with the thought that they con-
tain no expressions injurious to the young, or antagonistic to the
most rigid moralist.

The introduction was written by a life-long friend, and though
there may be sentiments in it too flattering to the author, still
out of respect to the writer we leave them untouched.

Perhaps few of our readers realize the difficulties we have
encountered in the production of this work; therefore, criticise not
too harshly, but treasure up whatever grains of wheat may be
found among the chaff.

                                              THE AUTHOR.

INTRODUCTION.

A LITTLE more than forty-two years ago the subject of this sketch was born in a little log cabin, on the bank of the River Thames, in the Province of Ontario. His father, George Ward, was, if we mistake not, a native of New York State, and a member of one of the most historic families on the American continent. The great ancestor of this family, so far as America is concerned, was the Rev. Nathaniel Ward, an English non-conformist minister, who was silenced by Archbishop Laud in 1631, for preaching against the tyranny of King Charles I.

Nathaniel Ward came to America, became one of the founders of Haverhill, Mass., and was the author of the first code of laws ever drawn up in New England. One of his descendants, General Artemas Ward, became prominent in the Revolutionary struggle. He commanded the militia for a time, and afterwards, when Washington was appointed to the command of the colonial armies, General Ward held the position of major-general under, and in rank was second to Washington only. Several others of the Ward family have become scarcely less noted, among whom may be mentioned Samuel Ward, delegate to the Continental Congress, and governor of Rhode Island for several years, and John E. Ward, U. S. minister to China.

But the genius of the family seems to have ever been of a literary turn, with a tendency for radicalism. Among the prominent members still living, may be mentioned William H. Ward, editor of the New York *Independent;* Rev. Henry Ward, D.D., of Buffalo, New York, and Julia Ward Howe, the noted poetess, lecturer and female suffragist.

Henry Ward Beecher and Harriet Beecher Stowe, author of "Uncle Tom's Cabin," are said to belong to this family on their mother's side.

About the year 1836 George Ward, then a young man, left his father's house in western New York, and like thousands of other young men, started to try his fortunes in the then wild regions of the West. His route lay through Western Canada, and there he tarried for a time, working as a millwright. There also he became acquainted with a young Canadienne, whom he married; and there also the subject of this sketch was born. Afterward George Ward came on to Michigan, where he died in 1850.

After a time his widow married, and, as in many instances, young Ward became dependent upon his own resources. Several of his father's relatives were living near, and they took some interest in the lad. He became a most industrious student; often in the dim light of fading day, by the blaze of a pine knot, or early in the morning, while others were sleeping, he was to be· found at his books.

An incident or two may not be out of place here illustrating traits of character. At the age of thirteen he spoke so rapidly and stammered so badly that few of his acquaintances could understand him.

Somewhere he had read of Demosthenes, and how he had cured his stammering by wearing a pebble in his mouth. Young Ward resolved to try it, and for more than three years he carried a smooth, flat pebble inside his cheek, until he had habituated himself to speak more slowly and plainly.

When a little more than fourteen years of age he learned that his father's grave was likely to be disturbed by improvements near it. He set out on a journey of over a hundred miles on foot, ascertained the facts, hired out to a farmer till he earned sufficient to buy the grave, and place a simple slab at the head of it. On his way home he stopped at a little corner grocery to buy some cakes and where, also, was kept a book store and circulating library. He saw a book which he liked, hired out two days to saw wood to pay for the book and then set out on his journey. The book was called "Young Man's Friend," ten lectures by Daniel C. Eddy. He determined to write a copy of the entire book, that. its words might be impressed on his memory. This he did in the next four months by rising at four o'clock in the morning. Aside from the instruction which he thus received, he became a correct speller in most common words and acquired that terse style of composition which is manifest in his writings. At the age of fifteen he had gathered quite a little library. At that time books were not as cheap or plentiful as now, and during the commercial crash of 1856-7, money was very scarce. He worked for a whole week in the broiling sun hoeing corn for his pocket-Bible, (which, he writes to us), he still has in good condition after nearly thirty years of continuous wear.

In 1856 he made the acquaintance of Stephen Wright, who afterwards became somewhat noted as the co-worker of Fred Douglass, in the work of negro emancipation. Wright had once been a slave, had perchased his own freedom, and acquired a liberal education. From Wright young Ward learned the beautiful art of phonographic short-hand, and Wright by his kindness won the esteem of the lad, and enlisted his sympathies in behalf of the enslaved race. Uncle Tom's Cabin had been published in 1853, and was begining to affect society. The stirring political events from 1856 to 1860: the rapid progress of the abolition party: the free-soil struggle in Kansas: the workings of the fugitive slave law: all, made a deep impression on the mind of young Ward.

In 1860 while working at the store of Thomas Currie, now of Detroit, he became acquainted with a young woman about two years younger than himself; and one of those romantic attachments sprang up that leave an influence for many years. In 1861, she died suddenly, and so great was the influence on the youth's mind, that his friends advised him to seek recreation. Accordingly he went to Shakopee, Minn., and resided with his father's sister. Her husband was at that time editor of the *Shakopee Argus*, and here his literary career, if it may be so called, commenced. Encouraged by his uncle he contributed articles, both in prose and rhyme, to that paper for several years, some of which have been quite extensively copied into other journals and books.

The studious habits of young Ward attracted the attention of Rev. Mr. Pond, then residing near Shakopee. Mr. Pond was at that time superintendent of Indian missions in the north-west, and as such he asked his youthful friend to undertake the task of missionary teacher to the Indians near Fort Snelling. While here he learned much of Indian character and customs, and here he wrote "Wynona" and "Minnehaha." That summer when the Hudson's Bay fur trader's trains came down from the far north-west, and he saw their quaint wooden carts, each drawn by a single ox; when he heard the wild tales of that far-off country, and remembered that he had an uncle there engaged in the fur trade, he determined to go north and taste the pleasures and pains of wild adventure.

But the climate of Hudson's Bay is not a pleasant one from October to May; and so, with returning summer he came back, just as the country was thrown into that terrible excitement follow-

ing the battle of Bull Run.   Then he did just what might have
been expected — became a volunteer soldier.   He was present at
the battle of Mill Springs, Ky., where his friend and comrade, Jas.
Isenhour, was shot by his side.   One night while standing sentry
he conceived the idea of that poem entitled Civil War, commencing:

> Rifleman, shoot me a fancy shot,
> Straight to the heart of yon prowling vidette.

When relieved of his duty, he, by the flickering lamp light, and
using a drum-head for 'a table, wrote out the poem on a piece of
brown paper, and sent it to his uncle at Shakopee.   He was under Buel's command when he marched to the relief of Grant at
Shiloh, or Pittsburg Landing.   The next letter to his uncle carried.
a copy of that piece entitled "Unknown Heroes."

At the battle of Stone River or Murfreesboro, he was severely
wounded by a piece of shell.   He recovered sufficiently to become
a hospital steward, and there he wrote, "Who Was He?" and "We
Have Drunk From the Same Canteen."   He was also a corres-
pondent of the *North-Western Christian Advocate*, under the *nom*
de plume of "Miles, a Soldier."   When the war was over he was
not only released, but also received a recommend from several
chaplains to study for the Christian ministry.

For a time he worked in the sash and door manufactory of
Palmer, Fuller & Co., of Chicago.   When he had accumulated
sufficient funds he devoted his whole time to study and Sabbath
school missionary work, under the supervision of Dwight L. Moody,
who had not then attained to celebrity, but was simply a plain
shop-keeper.   Chicago was then scarcely one-half the size it now
is.   That portion of the city which lies north of Chicago River was.
then a vast accumulation of shanties.   No schools or churches were
to be found in that vicinity until the Illinois Street and other missions were started..   In the Illinois Street Mission Ward became an

active Sabbath school teacher, and he afterwards held the position of superintendent of the large Maxwell Street Mission. In the meantime he had married, and a few years after his wife died, leaving one child. In 1872 Mormonism attracted his attention, and after reading considerable on that subject he embraced the teachings of Joseph Smith, much against the wishes of his early friends. I was well acquainted with much of his early life; he was under my instruction for nearly four years. Since he went to Utah I have only corresponded with him occassionally. When I knew him he was an energetic young man, a painstaking student, and a radical thinker and fighter of what he considered wrong, though somewhat too sanguine and too sensitive for his own good.

Respectfully,

THOS. HARDT, A. M.

St. Louis, Mo.,
    January, 1886.

BALLADS OF LIFE.

JARED BARNES' FIDDLE.

It's nigh on twenty years ago,
Since last I handled that old bow—
Sit closer to the fire, Joe,
    I don't mind tellin' 'bout it.
It's mighty curious, I'll allow,
And while I think upon it now,
It's kind o' like a dream, somehow,
    And maybe you will doubt it.

You see that fiddle hangin' thar,
And that old bow without the har?
If they could speak, but here we are,
    And that was twenty years ago!
'Twas pow'rful chill and cold that night,
Pitch dark, without a gleam o' light,
And road and fences hid from sight,
    Beneath the drifted snow.

My Betsy—well, you've heard 'em say
As how the poor girl left one day,
And maybe more, it's people's way
    To make such matters light.
She'd somehow gone all wrong, you see,
And acted strange and queer to me—
God knows how kind I tried to be!
    Her mind, it wasn't right.

It came at last! It hurt me, Joe!
It seemed so hard o' heart, you know,
To say that my poor girl must go
      Up to the 'sylum's walls!
But they thought best; and so, at last,
I held my heart down hard and fast —
It seemed 'twas colder than the blast,
      Or any snow that falls.

And so we went, 'twas in the Spring,
I wondered how the birds could sing!
I saw no joy in anything
      Along that road to town!
But stop, before we left, that day,
She smiled and laughed, and seemed as gay
As little children in their play,
      And took the fiddle down.

Yes, put the old bow in my hand —
I trembled, Joe, I couldn't stand;
It seemed I couldn't keep command,
      The honest truth to tell.
I sat down by the window, though,
And played — somehow — I scarcely know,
With that 'ere crooked, time-worn bow,
      The tune she loved so well!

       *   *   *   *   *

The summer passed and winter came;
And often, Joe, I called her name,
And listened for her voice, the same
      As in the days before;
Till one dark night of wind and snow —
I sat where you are sittin', Joe —
There came a loud and ringin' blow
      Right there against the door.

I let 'em in. "She's gone!" they said;
"What gone?" says I, "My Betsy dead?"
But Joe, 'twas worse than death—she'd fled
    From out the 'sylum's wall!
Alone, out in the blindin' snow,
My poor crazed girl! God help me, Joe;
But how I cussed 'em high and low—
    I cussed 'em one and all.

"*I'll go*," I said, "I'll *find* her, too,
I don't want help from sich as you,
Go back to town, she'll find *me* true,
    My girl that went so wrong!"
And then—the strangest thing of all—
I saw the fiddle on the wall;
Wrapped bow and fiddle in a shawl,
    And took 'em both along!

My horse was swift; but who could ride
In snow-drifts pilin' high and wide,
And 'gainst the blindin' storm beside,
    And darkness everywhere?
Somehow, at last, we seemed to take
The road that leads straight to the lake—
The very point I tried to make—
    It seemed that she'd be there!

I stopped, and shouted loud and long;
My voice seemed weak, the storm so strong!
I called my girl that had gone wrong,
    My Betsy, gone astray!
And Joe, at last I heard a cry!
I heard her voice, so close, so nigh,
I leaped into the snow breast high,
    And tried to break the way.

And then her voice was lost again.
I called and shouted, all in vain;
And, Joe, I think my own weak brain
    Was crazed—I couldn't tell—   *
Leastwise, I took that fiddle, Joe,
And in the storm I drew the bow,
And played it—how I'll never know—
    That tune she loved so well!

And didn't she answer, singin', too!
And comin' toward me straight and true!
I played the old tune squarely through,
    Until she touched my hand!
Until she sank upon my breast,
Poor, frozen girl! *You* know the rest.
My Betsy died—they say 'twas best,
    I've tried to understand!

   *   *   *   *   *   *

Not any sum in solid gold
Would buy that fiddle cracked and old,
Because its voice so surely told
    My Betsy where to go.
Ah, well! may be she sings that song
Up *there* where people don't go wrong;
But, Joe, I'm tired: I've watched so long
    That grave beneath the snow.

MARCH, 1867.

SLEEP OF THE SIX HUNDRED.

O'ER their devoted head,
While the words thundered,
Snugly and heedlessly
    Snored the six hundred.

Boldly he spoke and well,
All on deaf ears it fell,
Vain was his loudest yell.
    Volley'd and thundered.

Great was the preacher's theme,
Screwed on was all his scheme;
Neither with shout nor scream
Could he disturb the dream
  Of the six hundred.

Terrors to right of them,
Terrors to left of them,
Terrors in front of them,
  Hell itself plundered
Of its most awful things,
All those unlawful things
Weak-minded preachers fling
  At the dumbfounded.

Boldly he spoke and well,
All on deaf ears it fell,
Vain was his loudest yell,
  Volley'd and thundered;
For caring—the truth to tell—
Neither for heaven nor hell,
  Snor'd the six hundred.

Still with redoubled zeal,
  Still he spoke onward —
And in the wild appeal,
Striking with hand and heel,
Making the pulpit reel,
  Shaken and sundered;
Called them the Church's foes,
Threatened with endless woes;
Faintly the answer rose—
Proof of their sweet repose—
From the united nose
  Of the six hundred.

L'ENVOI.

Sermons of near an hour,
Too much for human power,—
Prayers, too, made to match,
(Extemporaneous batch,
    Woefully blundered).
With a service of music,
Fit to turn every pew sick,
    Should it be wondered?

Churches that will not move
Out of the ancient groove
    Through which they've floundered;
If they will lay behind,
Still must expect to find
Hearers of such a kind
    As the six hundred.

1871.

EVERMORE.

I BEHELD a golden portal in the visions of my slumber,
    And through it streamed the radiance of a never-setting day,
While the angels tall and beautiful, and countless without number,
    Were giving gladsome greeting, to all who came that way;
And the gates, forever swinging, made no grating, no harsh ringing,
    But melodious as the singing of one that we adore.
And I heard a chorus swelling, grand beyond a mortal's telling,
    And the burden of that chorus was Hope's glad word "Evermore."

And as I gazed and listened came a slave all worn and weary,
    His fetter links blood-crusted, his dark brow clammy, damp;
His sunken eyes gleamed wildly, telling tales of horror dreary,
    Of toilsome struggles through the night amid the fever swamp.

Ere the eye had time for winking, ere the mind had time for thinking,
An angel raised the sinking wretch and off his fetters tore.
Then I heard the chorus swelling, grand beyond a mortal's telling,
"Pass, brother, through our portal, thou'rt a freeman evermore."

And as I gazed and listened, came a mother wildly weeping:
"I have lost my hopes forever; one by one they went away;
My children and their father, the cold grave hath in keeping,
Life is but lamentation, I know not night nor day!"
Then the angel softly speaking: "Stay sister, stay thy shrieking;
Thou shalt find those thou art seeking, beyond that golden door."
Then I heard the chorus swelling, grand beyond a mortal's telling:
"Thy children and their father shall be with thee evermore."

And as I gazed and listened came one whom desolation,
Had driven like a helmless bark from infancy's bright land;
Who ne'er had met a kindly look—poor outcast of creation,
Who never heard a kindly word, nor grasped a kindly hand.
"Enter in; no longer fear thee; myriad friends are there to cheer thee;
Friends always to be near thee—there no sorrow sad and sore!"
Then I heard the chorus swelling, grand beyond a mortal's telling,
"Enter, brother, thine are friendship, love and gladness evermore."

And as I gazed and listened came a cold, blue-footed maiden,
With cheeks of ashen whiteness, eyes filled with lurid light;
Her body bent with sickness, her lone heart heavy laden—
Her home had been the roofless street, her day had been the night.
First wept the angel sadly, then smiled the angel gladly,
And caught the maiden madly rushing from the golden door;
Then I heard the chorus swelling, grand beyond a mortal's telling:
"Enter, sister, pure thou shalt be, and redeemed for evermore!"

I saw the toiler enter, to rest for aye from labor,
The weary-hearted exile there found his native land;
The beggar there could greet the king as an equal and a neighbor,
The crown had left the kingly brow, the staff the beggar's hand;

And the gate, forever swinging, made no grating, no harsh ringing,
But melodious as the singing of one that we adore;
And the chorus still was swelling, grand beyond a mortal's telling,
While the vision faded from me, with the glad word, " Evermore."

TIME BRINGS CHANGE.

THERE was a child, a helpless child,
Full of vain fears and fancies wild,
Who often wept and sometimes smiled
    Upon its mother's breast.
Feebly its meanings stammered out,
And tottered tremblingly about,
And knew no wider world without
    His little home of rest.

There was a boy, a light-heart boy,
One whom no trouble could annoy,
Save some lost sport or shattered toy
    Forgotten in an hour.
No dark remembrance troubled him,
No future fear his path could dim,
But joy before his eyes would swim
    And hope rise like a tower.

There was a man, a wary man,
Whose bosom nursed full many a plan
For making life's contracted span
    A path of gain and gold.
And how to sow and how to reap,
And how to swell his shining heap,
And how the wealth acquired to keep
    Secure within its fold.

There was an old, old grey haired one,
On whom, had four score winters done
Their work appointed, and had spun
    His thread of life so fine,
That scarce its thin line could be seen,
And with the slightest touch, I ween,
'Twould be as it had never been,
    And leave behind no sign.

And who were they, those four whom fate
Seemed as strange contrasts to create,
That each might in his different state
    The other's pathway shun?
I tell thee, that that infant vain,
That guileless boy, that man of gain,
That grey beard, who did roads attain
    So various — *they were one.*

MAY,. 1878.

LIFE.

WE build our puny works on beds of sand,
    Gilding the roughness with a film of gold,
The winds loosed from the hollow of His hand,
    Sweep o'er the temple, and the tale is told.

We climb the rugged steeps of earthly fame,
    Leaving sweet blossoms in the vale below,
And learn too late that on the upper height
    Is the cold glitter of eternal snow.

We watch and wait, we strive and hope in vain,
    For full fruition of our happy dream;
The mirage springs afresh, still further on,
    The golden apples are not what they seem. ·

We bear our crosses with too loud complaint,
    As if He could not hear who bore them first,
And with the paths wherein our footing treads,
    With stubborn blindness, oft we choose the worst.

Yet from His human heart, He dropped the seed
    That springs eternal in the deathless soul,
And the dim reachings of our feeble hands
    Are blossoms of the fruit that waits the goal.

And in the tender, erring heart He made
    With all its faults and burdens of regret,
The imprint of a perfect life is traced,
    The kingly seal upon its tablet set.

APRIL, 1878.

THE OLD MAN IN THE STYLISH CHURCH.

WELL, wife, I've been to church to-day—been to a stylish one—
And seein' you can't go from home, I'll tell you what was done.
You would have been surprised to see what I saw there to-day,
The sisters were fixed up so fine they hardly bowed to pray.

I had on these coarse clothes of mine—not much the worse for wear—
But then they knew I wasn't one they called a millionaire,
So they led the old man to a seat away back by the door,
'Twas bookless and uncushioned—a reserved seat for the poor.

Pretty soon in came a stranger with a gold ring and clothing fine,
They led him to a cushioned seat far in advance of mine.
I thought that wa'n't exactly right to seat him up so near,
When he was young, and I was old and very hard to hear.

But then there's no accountin' for what some people do,
The finest clothing nowadays of'n gets the finest pew,
But when we reach that blessed home, all undefiled by sin,
We'll see wealth beggin' at the gate, while poverty goes in.

I couldn't hear the sermon, I sat so far away,
So through the hours of service I could only "watch and pray;"
Watch the doin's of the Christians sittin' near me round about;
Pray that God would make them pure within as they were pure without.

While I sat there, a-lookin' upon the rich and great,
I kept thinkin' of the rich man and the beggar at his gate;
How, by all but dogs forsaken, the poor beggar's form grew cold,
And the angels bore his spirit to the mansions built of gold.

How at last the rich man perished, and his spirit took its flight
From the purple and fine linen to the home of endless night;
There he learned, as he stood gazin' at the beggar in the sky,
"It isn't all of life to live, nor all of death to die."

I doubt not there were wealthy sires in that religious fold
Who went up from their dwellings like the Pharisee of old,
Then returned home from their worship with a head uplifted high,
To spurn the hungry from their door with naught to satisfy.

Out, out with such professions! they are doin' more to-day
To stop the weary sinner from the gospel's shinin' way,
Than all the books of infidels, than all that has been tried
Since Christ was born in Bethlehem — since Christ was crucified.

How simple are the words of God, and yet how very grand,
The shells in ocean caverns, the flowers on the land,
He gilds the clouds of evenin' with the goldlight from his throne —
Not for the rich man only, not for the poor alone.

Then why should man look down on man because of lack of gold?
Why seat him in the poorest pew because his clothes are old?
A heart with noble motives, a heart that God has blest,
May be beatin' heaven's music 'neath that faded coat and vest.

I'm old—I may be childish—but I love simplicity,
I love to see it shinin' in a Christian's piety.
Jesus told us in His sermons, in Judea's mountains wild,
He that wants to go to heaven must be like a little child.

Our heads are growin' gray, dear wife—our hearts are beatin' slow,
In a little while the Master will call for us to go;
When we reach the pearly gateways, and look in with joyful eyes,
We'll see no stylish worship in the temple of the skies.

I WAS THINKING AS WE SAT HERE.

I was thinking as we sat here, dear wife,
     In the sunset's golden glow;
Of scenes long past in our early life,
     In the happy long ago.
Could I have my wish I would take you back,
     You would there be sitting now;
With not a care on your loving heart,
     Nor a wrinkle upon your brow.

The clock of Time should go back with you,
     All the years you have been my wife;
Till its golden hands just pointed out,
     The happiest hour of your life.
I'd wish it to stop at that glorious time;
     The clock should no longer run,
You would not be sad, and sick, and old,
     If to wish and to have were one.

I was thinking as we sat here, dear wife,
In the sunset's golden glow,
Of scenes long past in our early life,
In the happy long ago.

I would wish you there in the summer woods,
    Near your native sea-side town,
Our beautiful boy would play in the leaves,
    Or search for the nuts so brown.
In delight you would play and sing to him,
    No parent under the sun
Would have such a perfect child as yours,
    If to wish and to have were one.

And I would be there with you. dear wife,
    In the old home by the sea,
I would fly to you as the wild dove flies,
    To his mate in the forest tree.
Your brothers—one sleeps in the ocean deep,
    And one 'neath a tropic sun —
They'd both be there, young manly men,
    If to wish and to have were one.

I would have no toils, you would have no pain,
    Hope would banish all future dread,
Parents and brothers would live again,
    And our boy would not be dead.
I feel it all will come right at last,
    When our toils and tasks are done,
We shall dwell together in some good world,
    Where to wish and to have are one.

A CHILD'S IDEA.

WHAT beautiful beds the clouds would make!
    Softer than daintiest down,
Fold upon fold of delicate tints,
    And gold like a monarch's crown.

If I were an angel, I would choose
  The one of silvery white,
With crimson shading it just enough,
  To keep me warm in the night.

And when at eve, I had said my prayers —
  For I suppose angels pray —
I would cuddle me down in my cosy bed,
  And sleep till the "peep o' day.".

BE TRUE TO THYSELF.

BE true to thyself, in the right never falter,
  Though others prove false as a mirage in air;
Never swerve from the good, and time never can alter
  Thy peace by its sorrows, — thy love by its care.

Be true to thyself, cherish every affection
  That's gentle, and noble, and truthful, and pure,
And the strength of the Highest shall be thy protection,
  So long as thy love for thy God shall endure.

BE true to thyself, though the past, with its sorrow,
  And all its lost hopes, are remembered by thee;
Though the present be lonely, a brighter to-morrow
  May herald a future from sorrow set free.

Be true to thyself, and thy heart will forever
  Be true to all others; all truth is sublime;
Be true to thy God, and his goodness shall never
  Desert thee, through all the mutations of time.

MAY, 1878.

THE DESTINED WAY.

If to our fierce rebellious cries,
  Should guiding powers give way,
The flowery path that before us lies,
  So tempting and smooth, might stray
Into treacherous marshes or deserts drear,
  Or caverns dark where we'd cower with fear,
If perchance the voice of God we'd hear,
  Abroad at the close of day.

It is not always the paths that seem
  The smoothest that lead to rest;
It is not always the way we deem
  Most pleasant that proves the best;
For the path we must tread, but fain would shun
  Because of its roughness, may be the one
That shall lead our feet at the set of sun
  To the city of the blest.

1867.

THE LION'S BRIDE.

(FROM THE GERMAN).

For the bridal arrayed, with the wreath in her hair,
The keeper's young daughter, so rosy and fair,
In the lion's den stepped, with fawning and play;
At the feet of his mistress, the king of beasts lay.

The monarch beast once so intractable, wild,
At his mistress now gazes so knowing and mild;
The maiden so tender and winsome there stands,
Strokes the mane of the lion, tears fall on her hands.

♥'In the days that are past we were happy and gay,
Like play-fellows fond, like children at play,
We each other loved, each to other was kind;
But the days of our childhood we're leaving behind.

"Thy head so majestic, thy billowy mane,
How kingly thou lookest, I'll stroke thee again:
Time changes thou seest, thou'lt find me no more,
The child of the past or child-like as of yore.

"Oh, were I a child, and could stay here with thee,
My trusty, brave, honest, old fellow; we'd be
So happy; but I must now go far away,
To the land of the stranger, with strangers to stay.

"He met me, he wooed me, he said I was fair,
He won me, 'tis done, see the wreath in my hair.
My early companion with grief in my heart,
With tears in my eyes, farewell, we must part.

"Understandest thou all? Why looking so stern,
I am calm, in earnest, be calm thou in turn,
There, he's coming the one with whom life I shall spend,
This last kiss I give thee, farewell my old friend."

As the maiden rose up he looked sadly and grim,
The cage, it was shaking, he trembled each limb,
And when at the entrance the bridegroom he 'spied,
O, horrors! he grasped at the poor trembling bride.

At the door of the cage he stood as a guard,
He lashed his tail madly and loudly he roared;
She implores, she commands, she threatens; 'tis vain,
He stands at the gate, he is shaking his mane.

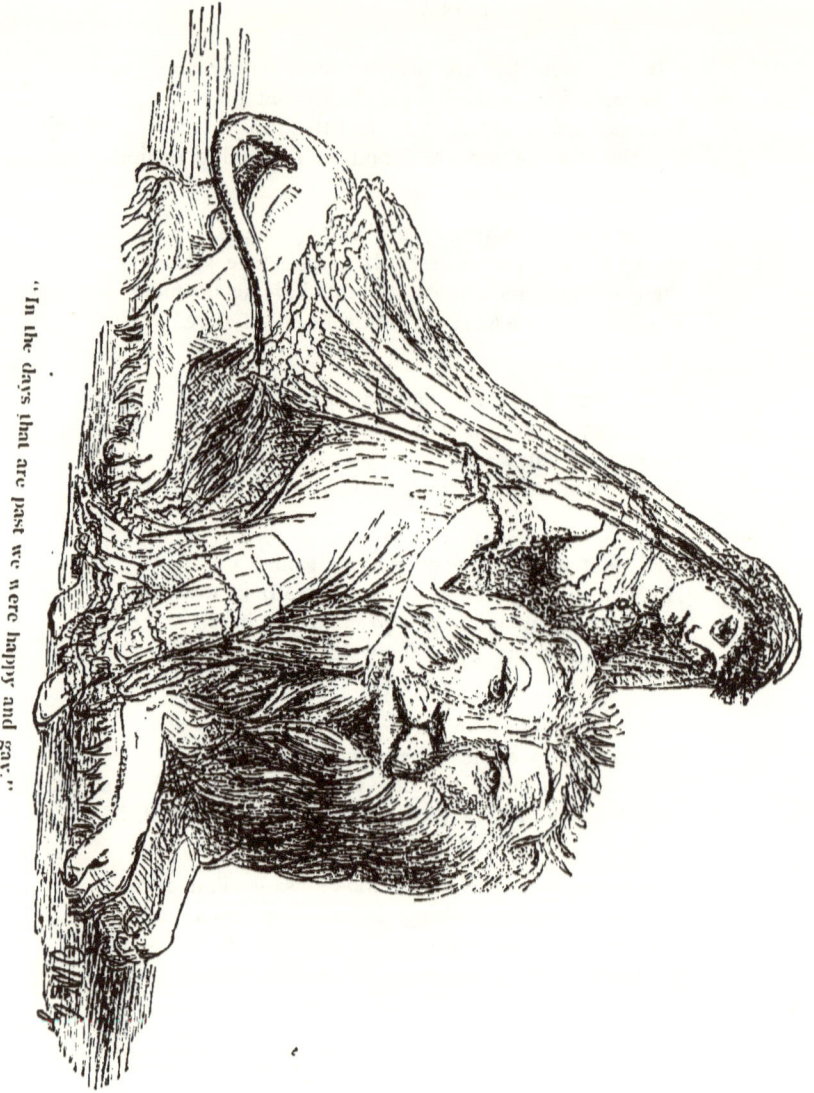

"In the days that are past we were happy and gay."

Outside shrieks of terror were rising from all,
The bridegroom cried, "Quick, bring gun, powder and ball,
The terrors to-day his life-blood shall assuage;"
The lion, excited, was foaming with rage.

At this moment the girl sprang swift for the door,
The lion transformed siezed her wildly and tore
That beautiful form, so lately caressed,
Lies bloody, distorted and dragged in the dust.

And as if forgotten the blood he had shed,
The lion laid gloomily down by the dead,
He lay there so sunken, by grief so oppressed,
Till the bridegroom a rifle-ball sent through his breast.

WANTED.

THE world wants men — large-hearted men,
    Whose hearts are raised from self above;
Who'll join the chorus and prolong
    The psalm of labor and of love.

The age wants heroes, who shall dare
    To stand for right when friends are few,
To hurl down wrong from its high seat;
    To the oppressed firm friends and true.

The time wants scholars who shall bear
    Opinion to a loftier place;
Shall shape the fate of dubious years,
    And herald in the dawn of peace.

Heaven wants fresh souls—not shrivelled ones,
 Fresh souls, my brother, give thine own;
So shalt thou prove thine heritage
And triumph when thy work is done.

So shalt thou be what scholars should,
 And walk the earth with hero's tread;
So shalt thou stand amidst the good,
 With God's bright aureole round thy head.

Thy heart shall seem a thousand hearts,
 Each heart with myriad raptures full,
Rich with the wealth that heaven imparts,
 The jewel of a ransomed soul.

DECEMBER, 1878.

SOLILOQUY OF A LOAFER.

SETH GRIMES and I were classmates once,
 And I was rich and he was poor;
I had—alas! it was my bane!—
 The wealth a father laid in store.

Seth toiled at morn, and noon, and night,
 Until his hands were hard and brown,
To pay his board and tailor's bills,
 While I was lounging round the town—

But mostly in the dry goods store
 To see the pretty girls come in,
Or smoking with my jolly peers,
 Who are the fools of "Auld Lang Syne."

The village belles looked proud and fierce
  If Seth made e'en the least advance;
And none, from *Inez* down to *Poll*,
  Would be his partner in the dance.

But I, half drunk with sparkling port,
  Waltzed with the fairest of the fair;
And "high born" Inez' proud papa
  Once asked what my intentions were!

Thus stood Seth Grimes and I at school;
  And yet on exhibition day,
Although the ladies praised me much,
  He, somehow, bore the *prize* away.

In brief, through long and weary nights,
  He stored his mind with knowledge rare,
And I—learned how to guzzle wine,
  And how to pick a good cigar.

Some three and thirty years have passed
  Since we on life's great sea set sail;
And lo! the beam is sadly turned
  In fortune's strange uneven scale.

My vaunted wealth has taken wings
  And flown away to parts unknown;
Indeed—with sorrow be it said—
  I'm on the *poor-list* of the town.

While Seth, who toiled to pay his way,
  Until his hands were hard and brown,
Is now receiving his reward
  As Senator at Washington.

A TERRIBLE TERRIER.

"FOUND, on Saturday last, between
Robinson Street and Jackson Green,
A Terrier Dog; owner's name
Not on the collar; owner of same
Can have by"—etc.

Yes, I *had* found a dog,
One night, when November's drizzle and fog
Were above and around, and under foot,
I stumbled over a draggled brute—
Kicked it away, and hurried on,
Thinking the muddy mop was gone;
It wasn't; I tried to dodge it; no—
Wherever I went the pup would go;
So the only method I could devise
Was to take it home—and advertise.

A week went past, and nobody came;
A month—two months; there wasn't a claim;
And so I determined at last to sell it,
And having determined, needs must tell it—
Ass that I was—to the women folk;
With one unanimous voice they spoke:
"What! sell wee doggie, the little pet!
And hadn't I come to love it yet?
The playful doggie! And somebody'd get it
Who'd scold and beat it, instead of pet it.
Surely, I hadn't the heart—I couldn't;
Besides, it was really wrong; I shouldn't!"

When women say *shouldn't*, always give in;
I always do; it saves my skin.

As on balanced chair the Senator swung,
Caught at the coat that so temptingly hung;
Looked round with a look indescribably knowing,
And pulled.

We kept the dog, and I rather guess
That a monkey insane would have plagued us less;
It ate the butter; it stole the meat;
It trod on books with its dirty feet;
It fought with the cat; it broke the bowls;
It grubbed the garden; it chased the fowls;
It leaped on the board when I played at chess;
I'd to pay for my wife's sublimest dress;
All mischief that ever dogs had done
Was bundled up in that single one.

'But the crowning mischief was at hand:
We gave a dinner, and gave it grand;
It pinched and plagued me for half a year
Getting things gorgeous and good—and dear,
For there was coming, in all his state,
A live Senator, awfully great.
The day of our dinner came at last,
And the dinner without a hitch went past;
We were terribly anxious not to offend,
For my wife had said, "We might make a friend—
Just think of a Senator such as he!"
But destiny willed that it shouldn't be.

We were talking; and there the Senator sat,
Speaking like Justice, and heard like Fate,
But beginning to thaw, like a man who had dined,
When that cursed terrier came up behind;
As on balanced chair the Senator swung,
Caught at the coat that so temptingly hung;
Looked round with a look indescribably knowing,
And pulled; the Senator felt himself going;
Gave a great start, and clutched at the table,
To keep from falling, but wasn't able;
And table-cloth over, and Senator under,
Down he went, with a crash like thunder.

Then stared the gentles and shrieked the dames;
I called the dog some unprintable names.
It stared at the mischief it had done,
Half in astonishment, half in fun.
Then — horror! — before the Senator rose,
It went, and, quite gravely, smelt of his nose;
Somebody tittered; more titters came after,
And then it ended in roars of laughter.

What endless methods we tried to assuage
The fallen Senator's smothered rage;
He turned it off with a careless joke;
But his smile was a quivering grin as he spoke.
He sat in his chair in most solemn *pose*,
And ever he furtively rubbed his nose.

The party broke up; the Senator went,
And for good; in vain invitations were sent;
In vain we visited; told our pain,
And flattered, by proxy — all in vain.
We tried him on every conceivable tack,
But the lost Senator never came back.

So all our hopes of greatness were reft;
But one consoling revenge was left;
I kicked the terrier out, and swore
I would never be plagued with a terrier more.

A STRANGE AFFAIR.

As I walked one evening over the lea,
A very strange (?) incident came to me —
A youth I saw near a woodland bight,
Up and down he rode in the evening light.

The moon shone calm on that summer scene —;
Now guess if you can what did all this mean?

The wild birds flew o'er the lovely spot,
The young man oblivious heeded not,
But he blew his horn by the forest green;
'Twas strange, who will tell me what could that mean?

And as I continued farther to roam,
A maid's sweet voice sang a song of home:
For a lonely maid in a tiny bark,
Went floating by in the coming dark.
While the fishes around her sportive play,
But what did the maid in the evening gray?
She sang a song by the forest green;
Now tell, if thou canst, what could that mean?

And as I returned in the evening fall,
The strangest (?) incident happened of all;
For a horse without rider stood near by,
And an empty boat on the beach was nigh.
And, passing the grove, what heard I there?
A walking, laughing, whispering pair,
The moon shone calm on that summer scene;
Now guess, if you can, what did all this mean?

O HEART OF MINE!

O heart
Of mine, look up;
Thy part
Hath been to sup
The cup
Of sorrow dry;
Look up
To clearer sky.

A haze,
Was round about;
A maze
And no way out.
A life
Was on the wane;
And strife
With God was vain.

And yet,
O heart of mine,
Forget;
Cease to repine.
Thy fears
Cease to recall;
And tears,
So idle all.

Sad heart
Of mine, be brave;
Thy smart
No power could save;
And yet,
Though crushed and bowed,
Forget
Not, thou art proud.

"And yet"—
My heart replied —
"Forget?
Oh no! My pride
Shall be
That God hath still,
With me
More power than will."

THE HAPPY ISLANDS.

HE roams about the town in dark or day,
  An old man with bent form, and long gray hair,
Whose eyes seem looking far and far away,
  As if in hope of seeing something there
Which he has looked for long, but cannot find.
  Among the busy crowd, he heeds it not,
And comes and goes, to all our pleasures blind.
  The world we live in he has quite forgot.

Sometimes he stops you in the hurrying throng,
  And asks of you, "Why do we sail so far?
I know, full well, the vessel's course is wrong,
  For further south the Happy Islands are.
But we are near them, for last night I heard
  The sound of voices coming from their shore,
And caught the scent of balm, and one bright bird
  Flew homeward, over us, to roam no more.

"I almost thought I saw them, in the dawn,.
  Fair as the sun-flushed peaks of Paradise,
But when the day broke fully they were gone;
  More to the south the land we seek for lies.
Pray God they turn the vessel ere too late!
  Must we sail by, and miss them as before?
They make mistakes, and lay it all to fate
  That we have never reached the longed-for shore."

And as he talks to you, the old man's eyes
  Are looking southward, where he hopes to see
The purple peaks, crowned with strange glory, rise
  'Neath fairer skies than those of Italy.

No sight of land to glad his weary eyes!
"Ah! we have missed them, as so oft before?
And oh! we were so near, so near!" he cries.
"Must we sail on and on forever more?"

Where are our Happy Islands? Must we sail
    Forever past them, when so near they seem?
Blow from the shores we left, oh, favoring gale,
    And waft us to the shores that haunt each dream.
Oh, voyagers with me, pray God we find
    The shores we seek, and do not pass them by!
Oh, blow us further south, inconstant wind,
    For there, we think, the Happy Islands lie!

THE THEOLOGICAL DISPUTE.

Written at the time of the dispute between Rev. Dr. Patton and Prof. Swing, of Chicago.

"You must keep," quoth the strict Dr. Patton,
"The straight Presbyterian hat on."
        "I shall do no such thing,"
        Said the liberal Swing:
"Sooner perish than always feel that on."

"Then vengeance," cried stiff Dr. Patton,
"Will spring, as a cat does a rat on;
        For the charges I bring,
        Will surely make you Swing!"
Then straightway his high horse he gat on.

The council then called by bold Patton,
The subject had many a chat on;
        But the charges fell flat,
        And so did the hat,
Which the council in wisdom, then sat on.

THE TIDE OF LIFE.

ALREADY on this ancient earth,
  Numberless peoples here have dwelt:
And offerings vast to gods been given,
  Around those altars myriads knelt.

In days to come religious souls,
  To God shall fairer altars rear;
And other pains and sorrows come,
  And other hopes men's hearts endear.

I am not dazed,— with loving looks,
  Time's awful whirl I gaze upon;
Midst varying tribes and changing realms,
  The stream of life flows grandly on.

I know that ne'er a day-dawn glimmered,
  But gladdened some poor lonely heart,
That never frost by spring was followed,
  But caused some sweet glad song to start.

From love of power, of right, of woman,
  Vast schemes are formed, inventions rise;
I know that in a woman's kisses,
  A strength for nobleness there lies.

The sailor leaves his home and darlings,
  For hopes of wealth beyond the sea;
The kiss of the laborer's wife at morn,
  Inspires with joy the livelong day.

I know the sky in every zone
  Is sometimes dark, then smiles so bright.
On starry constellations all,
  Believing eyes look up at night.

Thus ever I behold the same,
  In every human breast 'tis found;
We brothers are in every realm,
  Mine eyes have seen the wide world round.

A jot in vast creation's chain,
  That binds the past and future sphere,
I snatch from out Time's rolling surge,
  The pearl-drop of existence here.

TO AN OLD TIME FRIEND.

WHEN I met thee, gentle sister, in the days of long ago,
This world of our was fairer than it seemeth now, I trow;
The meadow grass was greener, the sky a deeper blue,
The stars of heaven seemed brighter—brighter every drop of dew.

The shining rills and rivers, sung a softer melody,
As they went arrayed in diamonds, to their bridal with the sea;
The birds made sweeter singing midst the summer-scented leaves,
Richer gold and crimson curtains hung around the dying eaves.

The winds dropped fonder kisses on the lips of fairer flowers,
And love wove fairy garlands, down the pathway of the hours;
The frosts and snows of winter overflowed with joy and glee,
There was laughter in the raindrops, there was laughter in the sea.

The kiss of the laborer's wife at morn,
Inspires with joy the livelong day.

O the charm, the joy of living, in the glory and the glow,
Of the days we left behind us, in the bloom of long ago;
The future may be pleasant, but it never can repay
The freshness, and the beauty, that the past has swept away.

We may understand in heaven, all life's sorrows, all its cost,
We may find amidst the angels, the loved ones we have lost;
But will they wear the semblance, of the same dear forms they wore,
When they faded from our vision to seek the hither shore?

Shall we know them by their voices, by their faces still so dear,
Will they clasp our hands and greet us, as they used to greet us here?
Faith answers to my yearning, "In some blessed world above,
Thy heart shall find its treasures, by the instincts of its love."

So in God's good grace believing, I trust and wander on,
Through the shadows of the twilight, to the glories of the dawn;
But, sometimes, in my dreaming comes a soft and soothing strain,
Trembling from the walls of heaven, I know the sweet refrain.

I hear again the footsteps that may come no more below,
And listen to the voices of the happy long ago;
Thus my weary heart is rested in the vision land of sleep,
One bright, delicious moment, but, alas, it wakes to weep.

O, the sky has lost its sunshine, the stars are dim and cold,
And the world, to me in seeming, is growing gray and old,
The fancy that beguiled me wears a fetter on her wing,
And the harp I touched to music, has many a broken string.

May thine, O, gentle lady, be a brighter, better way,
May Hope still walk beside thee as down flowery paths of May;
May it never faint, or fail thee in the hottest hours of noon,
But cheer and comfort, as it did, in the balmy days of June.

May storms ne'er shade thy spirit, nor mildew stain thy flowers,
May sweetest birds keep singing amid life's summer bowers;
May joy e'er dwell with duty, peace sit beside thy door,
Whate'er the past behind thee, may the days be bright before.

Yet the fairest rose that bloometh, some touch of blight will bear,
The strongest heart will sometimes faint, borne down by grief or care;
Life's sweetest cup is mingled with bitterest drops of gall,
And dreary, rainy days will come upon the paths of all.

But if all that seemeth lovely, unselfish, pure and good,
Respectful, true and tender, in full-orbed womanhood;
Might win the fairest human lot our Father could assign,
That peace, that joy, that portion fair, would certainly be thine.

A DAUGHTER'S LOVE AT FOURTEEN YEARS.

How majestic he looks, his fine light hair,
    I would with no one exchange,
Like the floss of silk so soft and clear,
    His locks in ringlets arranged.
Oft I stroke them and then he smiles so calm,
    And calls me his darling Grace;
They are not black, nor gold nor brown,
    Then what is the shade, now guess?

His bearing, his looks are those of a king,
    His majesty goes to my heart;
And when he frowns I tremble with fear,
    And sometimes the tear-drops start.
Again his features light up with a smile,
    As cheery as conscience clear;
Then I even love on the stool to kneel,
    And bathe his hands with a tear.

Sometimes in the evening's golden haze,
　At the garden gate I stand;
I see him coming amid the trees,
　And I go and take his hand.

I awoke this morn at the earliest dawn,
  In the sun's early light I hied,
And joyfully skipping took my way
  To the banks by the fountain's side.
I strawberries found like rubies bright,
  See how in the basket they smile;
I'll place them 'neath his plate out of sight,
  For he'll dine in a little while.

Sometimes in the evening's golden haze,
  At the garden gate I stand;
I see him coming amid the trees,
  And I go and take his hand;
He calls me his joy, his hope, his pride,
  Ofttimes he gives me a kiss;
For he is my father so true and tried,
  And I am his darling Grace.

A FALLEN ONE'S LAMENT.

Where is the promise of my years,
  Once written on my brow?
Ere errors, agonies and fears
Brought with them all that speaks in tears,
Ere I had sunk beneath my peers?
  Where sleeps that promise now?

Naught lingers to redeem those hours,
  Still, still to memory sweet!
The flowers that bloomed in sunny bowers
Are withered all, and evil towers
Supreme above her sister powers
  Of sorrow and deceit.

I look along the columned years
    And see life's riven fane,
Just where it fell, amid the jeers
Of scornful lips, whose mocking sneers
Forever hiss within my ears,
    To break the sleep of pain.

I can but own my life is vain,
    A desert void of peace;
I missed the goal I sought to gain,
I missed the measure of the strain
That lulls Fame's fever in the brain,
    And bids Earth's tumult cease.

Myself! alas for theme so¯poor,
    A theme but rich in fear;
I stand a wreck on Error's shore,
A spectre not within the door,
A houseless shadow evermore,
    An exile lingering here!

1867.

THE SEVEN AGES OF WOMAN.

INFANCY.

FIRST soft and helpless, innocent and mild,
Smiles in her nurse's arms the female child;
Fresh from her Maker's hands, all pure and fair,
Unstained by sin, unruffled yet by care;
A stranger in this world of ceaseless strife,
Lovely and passionless her dawn of life.

She too will be mamma, and lull to rest
The mimic baby on her infant breast;
She too will dress, will cherish and sustain,
And guard her darling from distress and pain.

CHILDHOOD.

Next see her seated at her mother's feet,
With eyes upraised, the glance of love to meet;
Speech partially unlocked, in silvery tone
She now essays to make her wishes known;
Now to explain her doubtful meaning, tries
With mingled eloquence of lips and eyes;
Here the first sorrows of the child begin —
The slumbering passions waken from within;
Each in its turn its growing strength reveals,
Anger, and love, and grief, she keenly feels.
She too will be mamma, and lull to rest
The mimic baby on her infant breast;
She too will dress, will cherish and sustain,
And guard her darling from distress and pain.
While plain to all, yet to herself unknown,
The future mother in each act is shown.
With graver look and melancholy air
She cons her lessons with reluctant care.
The book, the pen, the needle, all engage
The cares and troubles of the second stage.

MAIDENHOOD.

A third advances—plays and tasks are past,
And life's sweet summer brightly dawns at last;
Spring's lovely buds expand to fairest flowers,
And hope's enchantment gilds the sunny hours.
And, blind to all its shoals, and storms, and strife,
She enters on the treacherous waves of life.
Ah! sweet, confiding season! o'er your bloom
Why should the blight of sorrow cast a gloom!
The false will mock, the wicked treat with scorn
The noblest virtues which that life adorn;
The crowd shall mark with cold, invidious gaze,
And those will trample who should help to raise,

Till from the freezing glance of heartless pride
Its fair endowment's slighted worth will hide,
Or bitterer far! perchance is doomed to prove
The venomed shafts of unrequited love.
At first her gentle heart by slow degrees
Listens to love's appeal—the field, the trees,
All nature seems in loveliest aspect dressed.
Is there a purer bliss we mortals claim
Than lovers' walk in the calm vesper time?
O, happy hours! when free from carking care,
Eden returns to bless the young and fair.
She loves the moonlight and the evening hour,
The river's margin and the forest bower;
There wrapt in musing she delights to stray,
And nurse the dream that o'er her soul has sway.
Sometimes 'tis hers, by struggling pangs oppress'd,
To hide the thorns that rankle in her breast,
With dying hopes to combat thronging fears,
And find a sad relief in gushing tears.
This cannot last, and time with noiseless wing
Sweeps o'er her bosom and allays its sting,
And other hopes and calmer feelings brings.

WIFEHOOD.

Thus pass the first three stages of her life:
A fourth succeeds and sees her now a wife;
Yet not perchance of him who taught her heart
Its earliest love, or caused its keenest smart.
Forgetful of the wrong that has been given,
When happily wed she makes of home a heaven.
Man's nurse in sickness and his joy in health,
His aid in poverty, his pride in wealth.
Her heart the solace when his wounded mind
Flies for relief and finds it ever kind:
Where, when all fail him, he can still confide,

There wrapt in musing she delights to stray,
And nurse the dream that o'er her soul has sway.

Its faith, like gold, more pure the more 'tis tried.
Though storms without on every side increase,
They cannot wreck the home of love and peace
Which on the rock of duty firmly stands,
While strife and folly perish on the sands.

MOTHERHOOD.

But now a period still more blest shall come,
And crown with joy the calm delights of home;
The sweetest era of the female life,
Which makes a mother of the happy wife,
And adds new strength unto that holy tie
For human happiness ordained on high.
As round their board the olive branches spring,
And love's dear claimants on their parents cling,
The mother sees beneath her anxious eyes
Her lovely hopes in fair succession rise.
The youngest, cradled on her fostering breast,
Smiles its delights, and softly sinks to rest;
Another darling with bewitching grace,
Hides in the slumber's robe his cherub-face,
As archly wanton, full of infant glee,
He laughs aloud, and peeps mamma to see.
A third, more active, boldly climbs her chair
And pleads his right each fond caress to share;
While a fair girl, who hangs upon her arm,
Rich in each playful wile and early charm,
In lisping tones her earnest wish has told:
That on her lap the baby she might hold.
The happy mother on her infant train
Gazes with transport which amounts to pain;
A smile of rapture on her lip appears,
But her soft eyes o'erflow with tender tears—
Tears which e'en watching angels might approve,
The holy weepings of maternal love.

WIDOWHOOD.

Blest in her duties, calmly glide away
The busy hours of life's meridian day,
Till time, advancing o'er the dial, flings
A darker shade, and that sad epoch brings
That mournful stage of comfortless distress
Which sees her now in widowed loneliness.
Consumed with sorrow and oppressed with care,
Only by faith she sees a lot more fair;
Only, as her glance on her children falls,
Living for them she earthly hopes recalls
From mingled feelings, tears her eyes o'erflow,
Blending the mother's love. the widow's woe.
Her toils and cares for them, that interest dear,
E'en robs of bitterness the falling tear;
'Mid trials she is strengthened, and her mind
Bows to the will of heaven, calmly resigned.

OLD AGE.

Slowly but sure life's sands declining flow
In ceaseless course what now remains to show
Of woman's days, when all has passed away
That charmed the young, the thoughtless and the gay,
And the fair fabric totters in decay;
When youth, and health, and strength, and beauty's beam
Appear like traces of some distant dream,
Of which remembrance almost seems to fade.
E'en from herself, who fondly once surveyed
The bright possessions, and, in raptured tone,
Exclaimed exulting, "These are all my own."
Now reft of all — faint, feeble, pressed with age,
We mark the feelings in the last great stage;
The feverish hopes, the fears, the cares of life
No more oppress her with their torturing strife;

The youngest, crad'ed on her fostering breast,
Smiles its delights, and softly sinks to rest;
Another darling with bewitching grace,
Hides in the slumber's robe his cherub face.

The restless tumults of her heart, to-day
Have passed with beauty and with youth away;
She, like some traveler who beholds the sun
Sinking before him e'er his journey's done,
Regrets not now to lose its noontide power,
But hails the coolness of the coming hour,
And feels a holy and divine repose
Rest on her spirit in life's evening's close.
She in her children's children tastes again
Maternal pleasure and maternal pain;
To them imparts the knowledge years have given.
And points their hopes to soar with hers to heaven.
Although her eyes are dim in age's night,
Yet still more brightly burns the inward light,
Guiding her spirit by its sacred ray,
To cast its mortal thralls and cares away,
And wait its summons to eternal day.

•

THE PILGRIM AND HIS STAFF.

My grandfather sits in his old arm chair,
The locks on his brow are bleached and spare;
He has done with care and with labor done,
He calmly waits for life's setting sun.

His heart goes back to the days agone,
When the lights of his household around him shone;
But they have departed—alas! for him—
When the ear is heavy, the eye grows dim.

The wife of his youth in the grave lies low;
The turf by her side is unbroken now—
And he thinks of the season hastening on,
When his name shall be traced in the cold white stone.

But he trembles not, and his brow is calm—
For beneath the grave is a mighty arm,
Whose strength he proved when his years were few,
And the "guide of youth" to his age proves true.

The Bible speaks to his failing ear,
And its precious words are a joy to hear;
Its pages glow with a living light,
Like the shining "ladder" let down at night.

The blessed Word, like a tree whose leaves
In its freshness and beauty the spirit weaves,
To bind in life's spring-time, around the brow;
That Word is his crown of rejoicing now.

And thus as he waits at the Jordan's brim,
Where ninety summers have bloomed for him,
The "closer than brother" is by his side,
And his eye is fastened beyond the tide.

It is good thus meekly to watch and wait,
Till the Master calls from the pearly gate,
And, with lamp well-trimmed at set of sun,
Go in with the wedding garment on.

The peace of his spirit, O! who can tell,
Whose life's great harvest is garnered well?
Who has done with care and with labor done,
And calmly waits for life's setting sun.

She in her children's children tastes again
Maternal pleasure and maternal pain;
To them imparts the knowledge years have given,
And points their hopes to soar with hers to heaven.

SONGS OF HOPE AND MEMORY.

.

PASSING AWAY.

Passing away, so whispers the wind,
  As it treads its trackless course;
Passing away, doth the bright rill say,
  As it leaps from its crystal source.
All passing away on the stream of time
To oblivion's vale in a far off clime.
    Matter and man, we make no delay —
    To eternity's gulf we are passing away.

Passing away! e'en the forest leaves
  Are now growing yellow and sere;
And the sylvan bower and the wild wood flower
  Fade along with the fading year.
Oh! passing away, 'tis a desolate scene
When nature is robed in sombre sheen,
    And the winds through the leafless forests bay
    With their dismal dirge: we are passing away

Passing away! mark the furrowed brow
  And the head with the silvery hair,
And the furrowed cheek, how they plainly speak,
  They're leaving a world of care,
Yes, passing away, even beauty's flower
Is fading fast 'neath the spoiler's power;
    And fair and frail, to their bed of clay
    Adown in the tomb are passing away.

Passing away! sounds the ocean wave,
    As it breaks on the beaten shore,
And the tortured tide is left to chide
    The cliffs with their hollow roar.
Aye, passing away! both from castle and cot,
The places which know us, will soon know us not;
      Whether peasant or prince, nature's last debt to pay,
      At the fiat of God, we are passing away.

Passing away; for their hour is past,
    Earth's things, they're a motley pyre;
The monarch's throne and his sword and crown,
    Wealth, fame and the poet's lyre.'
All passing away, e'en the pomp of art
And the pride of the despot must all depart,
      And the relics of realms must each decay,
      And the names of their great ones shall pass away.

Passing away! even Time himselt
    Bends under his load of years;
His limbs are frail, and his cheek grows pale
    With the furrows of sorrowing tears;
With his broken scythe, with a silent tread,
He is passing on to the home of the dead;
      With a bending form and locks grown gray.
      Old Time himself is passing away.

Passing away! how swiftly they go!
    Those scenes of our youth once dear,
Those friends we loved are by death removed,
    And the world grows strange and drear;
And the hopes of our youth so oft depart,
And the chords of love round the human heart;
      E'en the spirit grows tired of its cot of clay,
      And the essence immortal would fain pass away.

Passing away! all but God's bright throne
    And His children's home of love;
And His grace divine and the boundless mine
    Of God's eternal love.
But change shall yet come on rainbow wings,
And shall brighten the earth with happier things;
    Though suns and stars should all decay,
    Yet God in His love shall ne'er pass away.

RETROSPECTION.

I NOTE this morning how the sunshine falleth,
    Just as it fell one morning long ago.
A white dove walks the window-ledge, soft cooing;
    The waters murmur in their ebb and flow.

The aspen whispers to the autumn breezes;
    I see the golden rod on sloping hills;
I catch the odors of the brown leaves dying,
    And hear the babble of the shrunken rills.

I listen to some notes of children's laughter,
    Smiling to think how late I was a child—
A happy elf, with cheeks of sun-kissed crimson,
    And curls of tawny gold, wind-tossed and wild.

I see and hear; I know I am not dreaming;
    And still, somehow, I can not make it seem
But that I sleep, and see and hear things dimly,
    As one does often in a troubled dream.

Ah, well! what matter, since so soon for all
    Our toiling and our tears will have an ending,
And our tired hearts and hands shall rest for aye
    In that blest land to which our feet are tending.

AT REST.

From purple skies, my darling, the silver stars look down
O'er lonely field and meadow, and the quiet sleeping town;
And the winter's suns have drifted o'er the autumn's gold and red,
Till the heavy vines were drooping and the amber leaves were dead.
And many winds of winter have beaten wood and wave,
Till the river ceased to murmur and the year was in its grave—
With years so full of sunshine, so full of love and light,
Above whose withered roses my heart keeps watch to-night.

Across the heath, my darling, the starry lights are low,
And shadows rising, falling, like phantoms come and go,
As o'er the mossy woodland the fresh, sweet breezes play
Above the sleeping blossoms of many a sunny May;
And out across the meadow-land our feet so oft have pressed,
The ivy creeps above your head, no storm disturbs your rest;
While distant bowers grow still and lone, for swallows on the wing,
And o'er the dreary hills' appear the gentle dawning spring.

The tide of years, my darling, ebbs silently and fast;
It floweth on to meet the sea, so dark, so deep and vast;
Its song falls gently on my ear across the winter's snow,
And wakes the days that sleep for aye, the sunny long ago.
My heart forgets the monody by saddened memory sung
O'er buried fancies of a life no longer fair and young.
The breeze that wakes the snow drop from sleep within the wold,
Brings sweet perfume from flowers that grew in sunny fields of old.

The flowers that died, my darling, will raise their heads again,
Where drifts the golden sunshine across the weary plain.
The pleasant, dreamy days will come with roses newly blown,
As sweet and fair as those we knew in happy summers flown.

But dearer far, my darling, than all things else can be,
The hope that we shall meet again when I have crossed life's sea;
No wish of mine would wake you from rest so calm and deep,
No yearning break your sweet repose in peaceful, dreamless sleep.

But dearer far, my darling, than all things else can be,
The hope that we shall meet again when I have crossed life's sea;
No wish of mine would wake you from rest so calm and deep,
No yearning break your sweet repose in peaceful, dreamless sleep.

THE INCARNATION. ·

Hail to the night when erst on Judah's plain,
    A glittering host proclaimed a Savior come;
Not in the gorgeous pomp of kingly train,
    But meekly to this world of sin and gloom;
Not in Thy dread omnipotent array,
No indignation burned before Thee on Thy way.

For Thou wast born of woman meek and mild,
    And in the manger rude was laid to rest;
Earth had no place for Thee, O Heavenly Child,
    Though earth by Thee alone was truly blest.
Angels, not men proclaimed Thy mission here
And yet for man alone Thou shedst Thine every tear.

For man alone was every sorrow borne:
    Hunger, and thirst, and weariness, and pain;
For man alone Thy sacred flesh was torn,
    That sinful man might bless eternal gain,
Awhile the world grew dark for what was done,
Then basked in sweet repose beneath a cloudless sun.

No clouds of vengeance lowered when in Thy tomb
    Thy weeping followers laid Thee, Holy One,
Soon camest Thou forth fresh in immortal bloom!
    Angelic servants rolled away the stone.
Thy work accomplished, slowly didst Thou rise,
Calmly· majestic, Godlike to Thy native skies.

AN OLD MAID'S RETROSPECTION.

READING, PA., Feb. 3, 1885.—Undoubtedly the strangest character in Eastern Pennsylvania died to-day in the mountains back of Bernville. This was Sallie Kettner, known as the woman hermit of the mountains. When she took up her solitary abode she was thirty-six years of age. The story goes that in her youthful days she was the promised bride of a sailor, who was impressed into the French service and died in prison. On her bosom, when the dead woman was found, was the last letter from her lover, faded with age, written just before he died.

I LOOK into the dreamy past and see—what do I see?
They look like visions now, but then,—how real they were to me;
I see my girlhood full of hope, my lover true and brave;
In fancy still I hear his vow, as pledge of love he gave—
It was a ring; he smiling said, "'Twill serve to guard the space
Upon thy finger, till I put another in its place."
That first love-gift, see here it is—Oh, what a slender band,
Though tethered by a golden chain to this poor withered hand.

And it was in that girlish time, when I perchance might see
A youthful mother's glance of pride at babe upon her knee;
I envied her that happiness, and Oh, my heart beat wild,
That I might one day be his wife, and mother of his child.
'Twas woman's nature in me spoke, but scarcely had the thought
Been formed, ere maiden pride and shame a mingled color brought;
Vain was the guiltless blush, for though these hopes of mine might seem
So near fulfilment then, alas, they proved indeed a dream.

To win a home my lover true sailed from his native bay,
By tyrants seized, he lingered long in prisons far away;
Years passed—he wrote that silver threads were mingling with his hair;
They were in mine—those fruits, sown by the hand of Care;
Now whiter than the snow-clad hill or foam that crests the wave,
Are my thin locks; his weary head rests in a foreign grave.
Ay maidens, you may sigh, God grant that happier be your lot;
For me no power could make me wish this true love dream forgot.

But after all my pains, my fears, my visions of the past,
One ever-present hope of mine will be fulfilled at last;
And I am happy, for I know my bridal draweth nigh —
A union purer, holier far, in realms beyond the sky.
In every dream, by night and day, I hear again his voice
I fancy that he beckons me and calls me to rejoice;
That, when my eyes are closed in death, my truly loved will be
The first by the Eternal sent, to meet and welcome me.

COMPENSATION.

THE truest words we ever speak
    Are words of cheer.
Life has its shade, its valleys deep;
But round our feet the shadows creep,
    To prove the sunlight near.
Between the hills those valleys sleep —
    The sun-crowned hills!
And down their sides will those who seek
With hopeful spirit, brave though meek,
    Find gently flowing rills.

For every cloud, a silver light;
    God wills it so.
For every vale, a shining height;
A glorious morn for every night;
    And birth for labor's throe.
For snow's white wing, a verdant field;
    A gain for loss:
For buried seed, a harvest yield;
For pain, a strength, the joy revealed.
    A crown for every cross.

THE GOOD TIME NOW.

HUMANITY, with a mighty hope,
    Is watching with anxious eyes.
To see the light of a golden age
    On a waiting world arise.
Though weary and long may seem that time,
    Who under life's burden bow,
Yet progress is marching with steps sublime—
    'Tis even a good time now.

What better time could be ever sought
    For victories to be won
Than this earnest age with its noblest thought,
    And the work that should be done?
Earth's heroes all toiled thro' long, dark years
    Ere they saw life's fruited bough,
And the seeds of the harvest of future years
    Must be sown in the active now.

The sun is as bright that shines to-day
    As it will aye from hights sublime;
And God has as weighty words to say
    As to seers in ancient time:
Bright visions still come to faith's clear eye,
    To those who in meekness bow;
The pure behold the triumph nigh
    By the light of the good time now.

This living present, this longed-for hour,
    Is the one to us the best,
And the soul that uses its gift of power
    Shall evermore be blest.

Great souls by eternal truth set free,
No longer in shackles bow:
The midnight is past, the jubilee
Has begun with the good time now.

THE SPIRIT'S CRY.

O, MY Father whom angels environ,
    One gift from Thy bounty impart;
Not for wings nor for sinews of iron,
    I ask but Thy life in my heart.
I walk in the darkness and blindly,
    There's no one to teach me the right,
E'en my queries none answer me kindly—
    Thou only canst lead me to light.

From Thee I derived my existence;
    To Thee I return at Thy will—
I but ask Thee for strength and assistance,
    Thy law and my task to fulfill.
Give me strength, O Strong One and tender,
    The wisdom that comes from above:
Grief has taught me that none else can render
    What we need for life's labor of love.

In life's sorrows no more I'll be lonely,
    In conflicts no more be afraid;
I shall triumph, and triumph, aye only,
    If Thou wilt but give me Thine aid.
Let me lean on Thy bosom, O Strong One,
    O, Wise One, I am not afraid:
For I know that Thou never wilst wrong one
    Of those whom Thy goodness hath made.

THE COMING DAY.

LET Saints rejoice, the night is past,
The gospel day has dawned at last;
Soon shall the sun of righteousness
With healing wings the nations bless.

CHORUS: Hail to the coming morning,
And a future calm and bright!
Hail to the rosy dawning
Of the gospel's glorious light!

Let all obey the Lord's command
To spread the truth in every land,
Till all who dwell in error's night
Shall learn of Him and dwell in light.

Redeemed to God each land shall be,
And every island of the sea,
All nations learn to know the Lord
And live obedient to His word.

O speed the years and bring that day
When sorrow shall be done away:
When in the Savior's peaceful reign
Earth shall her long lost Eden gain.

A WAY I KNEW NOT.

'Tis not the way that lay so bright before me,
    When youth stood flush'd on Hope's enchanted ground;
No cloud in skies of azure bending o'er me,
    No desert spot in all the landscape round.

Fair visions, glimmering through the distance, beckon'd
My buoyant steps along the sunny way;-
Sweet voices thrill'd me, till I fondly reckon'd
That life would be one long blue summer day.

This was the path my feet had gladly taken;
And, blindly lured by that deceitful gleam,
I would have wander'd on, by God forsaken,
Till death awoke me from a fatal dream.

Alas! in youth by Eden's gate we linger;
In its green bowers we fain would make abode,
Till the stern Angel-Warder, with calm finger,
Points the feet outward to the desert road.

My pleasant path in sudden darkness ended,
My footsteps slipped, my hopes were well-nigh gone;
I could but pray,—and as my prayer ascended,
Thy face, O Father! through the darkness shone.

And by that light I saw the Cross of trial,
The landmark of the way my Savior went,—
The upward path of pain and self-denial;
And thou didst point me to the steep ascent.

A way I knew not—winding, rough, and thorny;
So dark at times I scarce the path could see;
But thou hast been my guide thro' all the journey,—
Its steepness has but made me lean on Thee.

And onward still I go, in calm assurance
That thou wilt needful help and guidance lend;
That strength will come for every day's endurance,—
Grace all the way, and glory at the end.

WRECKS.

Sunset's soft flush has faded
Out of the western sky,
And over the busy city
The twilight shadows lie.

A soft gray mist is spreading
O'er the lake and the distant land,
And white-capped waves come rolling,
To break on the pebbly strand.

The lamps in the street are lighted,
And the lamps in the vaulted blue,
While the rose-bud holds up her fragrant lips
To be kissed by the falling dew.

I stand in the twilight gleaming,
In the midst of the water's roar,
And think of my boyhood dreaming
That comes back to me nevermore.

There are wrecks on the beach by the headland,
And the sailors sleep under the waves;
No bell ever tolled for their funeral rites,
No prayers have been said by their graves.

Sad? I know of a thing that is sadder still —
Of a life that is wrecked and lost;
Of a brave proud heart that is struggling on,
Driven and tempest-tossed.

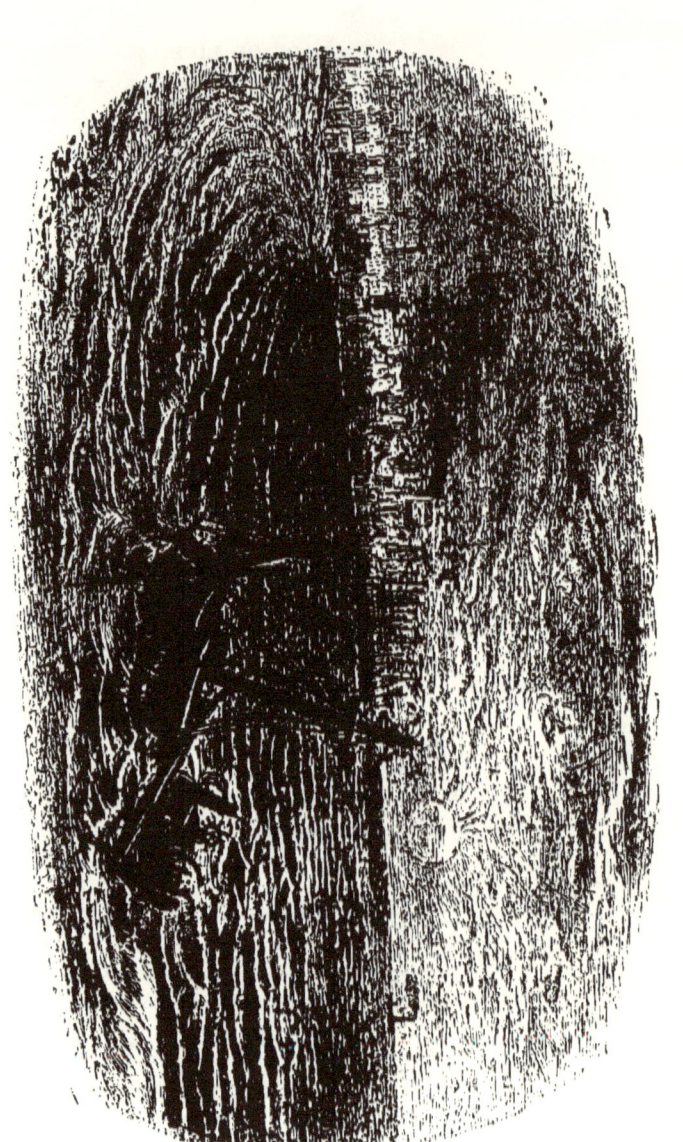

There are wrecks on the beach by the headland,
And the sailors sleep under the waves.

I know of a heart that strove and broke,
　　Of a conquered and humbled pride ;
Of a spirit that, tortured, crushed and wronged,
　　Wrestled and moaned and died.

I know — pshaw! what do you care?
　　Be still! I will tell no more,
But this: there are sadder wrecks by far,
　　Than the wrecks by the blue lake's shore.

CHICAGO, 1870.

HEAVEN.

BEYOND the chilling winds and gloomy skies,
　　Beyond death's cloudy portal,
There is a land where beauty never dies,
　　And love becomes immortal.

A land whose light is never dimmed by shade,
　　Whose fields are ever vernal;
Where nothing beautiful can ever fade,
　　But blooms for aye, eternal.

We may not know how sweet the balmy air,
　　How bright and fair its flowers;
We may not hear the songs that echo there,
　　Through those enchanted bowers.

The city's shining towers we may not see,
　　With our dim earthly vision;
For death, the silent warder, keeps the key
　　That opes those gates elysian.

But sometimes when adown the western sky
    The fiery sunset lingers,
Its golden gates swing inward noiselessly,
    Unlocked by unseen fingers.

And while they stand a moment half ajar,
    Gleams from the inner glory
Stream brightly through the azure vault afar,
    And half reveal the story.

O land unknown! O land of love divine!
    Father all-wise, Eternal,
Guide, guide these wandering, way-worn feet of mine
    Into those pastures vernal.

1860.

"A LITTLE WHILE."

OH! for the peace which floweth as a river,
    Making life's desert places bloom and smile!
Oh! for the faith to grasp heaven's bright "forever,"
    Amid the shadows of that "little while!"

"A little while" for patient vigil-keeping,
    To face the storm, to wrestle with the strong;
"A little while" to sow the seed with weeping,
    Then bind the sheaves and sing the harvest song.

"A little while" to wear the robe of sadness,
    And toil with weary step through miry ways;
Then to pour forth the fragrant oil of gladness,
    And clasp the girdle round the robe of praise.

"A little while," midst shadow and illusion,
    To strive, by faith, life's mysteries to spell;
Then read each dark enigma's bright solution,
    And hail sight's verdict, "He doth all things well."

"A little while" the earthen pitcher taking
    To wayside brooks, from far-off fountains fed;
Then the cool lip its thirst forever slaking,
    Besides the fullness of the fountain-head.

"A little while" to keep the oil from failing,
    "A little while" faith's flickering lamp to trim;
And then the Bridegroom's coming footsteps hailing,
    To haste to meet Him with the bridal hymn.

Thus He who is Himself the gift and giver,
    The future glory, and the present smile,
With the bright promise of the glad "forever,"
    Can light the shadows of the "little while."

1867.

TIRED OF PLAY.

Tired of play! Tired of play!
What hast thou done this livelong day?
The birds are silent and so is the bee,
The sun is creeping up steeple and tree;
The doves have flown to the sheltering eaves,
And the nests are dark with the drooping leaves;
Twilight gathers and day is done—
How hast thou spent it, restless one?

Playing? But what hast thou done beside,
To tell thy mother at eventide?
What promise of morn is left unbroken?
What kind word to thy playmate spoken?
How with thy faults has duty striven?
Whom hast thou pitied, and whom forgiven?
What hast thou learned by field and hill,
By greenwood path and by singing rill?

There will come an eve to a longer day,
That will find thee tired,—but not of play;
And thou will lean, as thou leanest now,
With drooping limbs and aching brow,
And wish the shadows would faster creep,
And long to go to thy quiet sleep;
Well were it then, if thine aching brow
Were as free from sin and shame as now.

Well for thee if thy lips could tell
A tale like this, of a day spent well;
If thine open hand hath relieved distress,
If thy pity hath sprung to wretchedness;
If thou hast forgiven the sore offence,
And humbled thy heart with penitence;
If nature's voices have spoken with thee,
With her holy meanings eloquently.

If every creature hath won thy love,
From the creeping worm to the brooding dove;
If never a sad, low-spoken word,
Hath plead with thy human heart unheard;
Then, when the night steals on, as now,
It will bring relief to thine aching brow;
And, with joy and peace at the thought of rest,
Thou wilt sink to sleep on thy mother's breast.

WE ARE GROWING OLD.

WE are growing old — how the thought will rise
    When a glance is backward cast,
On some long-remembered spot that lies
    In the silence of the past;   •
It may be the shrine of our early vows,
    Or the tomb of early tears,
But it seems like a far-off isle to us
    In the stormy sea of years.

O wide and wild are the waves, that part
    Our steps from its greenness now;
Ah, we miss the joy from many a heart
    And the light from many a brow;
For deep o'er many a stately bark
    Have the whelming billows rolled,
That steered with us from that early mark;
    O! friends, we are growing old.

Old in the dimness and the dust
    Of our daily toils and cares;
Old in the wrecks of love and trust,
    Which our burdened memory bears;
Each form may wear to the passing gaze
    The bloom of life's freshness yet,
And beams may brighten our later days,
    Which the morning never met.

But, ah! the changes we have seen
    In the far and winding way;
In our paths, the graves that have grown green
    And the locks that have grown gray;

7

Life's winter still on our heads may spare
    The sable or the gold,
But we see its snow upon brighter hair,
    And, friends, we are growing old.

We have gained the world's cold wisdom now,
    We have learned to pause and fear;
But where is the genial youth, whose flow
    Was a joy of heart to hear?
We may have won wealth from many a clime,
    And lore from many a page,
But where is the hope that saw in Time
    But its boundless heritage?

Will it come again when the violet wakes,
And the woods their youth renew?
We have stood in the light of sunny brakes,
When the sky was deep and blue;
And our souls might joy in the spring-time then,
Now joy without faith is cold;
Heaven only can give us our youth again,
And hearts that ne'er grow old.

THE TRIUMPH OF TRUTH.

IMPULSES fresh and pure to-day
From heaven inspire the human soul,
While time-worn errors pass away,
Nor longer minds of men control;
Blind superstition, cowering, hides
Amidst the ruins of the past,
Tradition hoary only bides
Where mental night's deep gloom is cast.

Churches in truth, no longer grand,
They pamper pride and wink at sin,
Like whited sepulchres they stand,
Holding but dead men's bones within;
Dry catechisms, forms and creeds,
And useless dogmas, old and new,
Are not the things for human needs,
With life's progression full in view.

Beyond these clouds of toils and tears,
As yet unseen by mortal eyes,
Great stars of Truth in other years
Shall yet illuminate the skies;
Brave souls who've toiled and waited long,
Amidst the tempest and the night,
Shall find redress for every wrong —
Shall find a friend for every right.

Truth triumphs, — e'en now wanes the night —
Soon will the morn reward our zeal;
Greater than man controls the fight,
For Truth is stronger far than steel.
Through every land with winged speed,
We only wish that Truth may go
From north to south; in very deed,
Truth is the best of guards we know.

Though hell's dark host opposing nears,
Upon the plain in armor now,
Truth bursteth through a thousand spears;
The laurel ever crowns his brow,
Who, armed with Truth, will hold at bay
The world; and crushed the despot's rods;
What if men now condemn my lay —
The triumph comes, the days are God's.

CHANCE.

A WORD unspoken, a hand unpressed,
A look unseen or a thought unguessed,
And souls that were kindred may live apart,
    Never to meet or know the truth —
Never to know how heart beat with heart
    In the dim past days of a wasted youth.

She shall not know how his pulses leapt
When over his temples her tresses crept;
As she leaned to give him the jasmine wreath
    She felt his breath, and her face flushed red
With the passionate love that choked her breath,
    And saddens her life now her youth is dead.

A faded woman who waits for death,
And murmurs a name beneath her breath;
A cynical man who scoffs and jeers
    At women and love in the open day,
And at night-time kisses, with bitter tears,
    A faded fragment of jasmine spray.

MINNE-HA-HA.

IN the land of the Dacotahs
    Flows a clear and sunlit stream —
Minnehaha, Laughing Water,
    Sporting in the morning beam
Echoing in the midnight stillness,
    Shivering in the morning ray,
Sparkling in the golden sunset,
    Laughing at the close of day.

In the land of the Dacotahs
    Flows a clear and sunlit stream —
Minnehaha, Laughing Water,
    Sporting in the morning beam.

By this stream of Indian romance,
　　Dark-eyed maids and warriors dreamed ;
Roamed the fair with Hiawatha,
　　Where the tiny rainbow gleamed ;
There they roamed as lovers only,
　　Listening unto Nature's tome,
Ere the beautiful Wynona
　　Hastened to the spirit home.

Gone are they, still Minne-ha-ha,
　　Laughing, shivering, dances on ;
Time, like thee, is swiftly passing —
　　Like thy bubbles, we are gone.
Still I linger as I leave thee,
　　That thine image e'er may stand,
Uneffaced, on memory's tablet —
　　Picture of that northern land.

SEPTEMBER, 1861.

A HOME PICTURE.

THE hearth is swept—the fire is bright,
　　The kettle sings for tea;
The cloth is spread, the lamp is light,
The muffins smoke in napkins white,
　　And now I wait for thee.

Come, home, love, come, thy task is done;
　　The clock ticks listeningly;
The blinds are shut, the curtain down,
The warm chair to the fireside drawn,
　　The boy is on my knee.

Come home, love, come; his deep fond eye
    Looks round him wistfully,
And when the whispering winds go by,
As if thy welcome step were nigh,
    He crows exultingly.

In vain—he finds the welcome vain,
    And turns his glance on mine,
So earnestly, that yet again
His form unto my heart I strain,
    That glance is so like thine.

Thy task is done—we miss thee here;
    Where'er thy footsteps roam,
No heart will spend such kindly cheer,
No beating heart, no listening ear,
    Like those who wait thee home.

Ah, now along the crisp walk fast
    That well-known step doth come;
The bolt is drawn, the gate is past,
The babe is wild with joy at last—
    A thousand welcomes home.

HUNGERING HEARTS.

SOME hearts go hungering through the world
    And never find the love they seek;
Some lips with pride or scorn are curled
    To hide the pain they may not speak;
The eyes may flash, the lips may smile,
    The voice in giddiest mirth may thrill,
And yet beneath them, all the while
    The hungry heart is pining still.

These know their doom, and walk their way,
   With level steps and steadfast eyes,
Nor strive with fate, nor weep nor pray;
   While others, not so sadly wise,
Are mocked by phantoms evermore,
   And lured by seemings of delight,
Fair to the eye, but at the core
   'Holding but bitter dust and blight.

I see them gaze from wistful eyes, . .
   I mark their sign on fading cheeks,
I hear them breathe in smothered sighs,
   And note the grief that never speaks;
For them no might represses wrong,
   No eye with pity is impearled;
Oh, misconstrued and suffering long,
   Oh, hearts that hunger through the world.

For you does life's dull desert hold
   No fountain's shade, no date grove fair,
No gush of waters clear and cold,
   But sandy reaches wide and bare.
The foot may fail, the soul may faint,
   And weigh to earth the weary frame;
Yet still, ye make no weak complaint,
   Nor speak a word of grief or blame.

Oh, eager eyes which gaze afar,
   Oh, arms which clasp the empty air;
Not all unmarked your sorrows are,
   Not all unpitied your despair.
Smile patient lips, so proudly dumb—
   When life's frail tent at last is furled
Your glorious recompence shall come,
   Oh, hearts that hunger through the world.

1865.
7*

UTAH, THE QUEEN OF THE WEST.

THE youth of each land for their fatherland stand,
　And boast of its grandeur with pride;
Whate'er their estate, their fortunes or fate,
　To none is this freedom denied;
Then why should not we, young, happy and free,
　Rejoice in the land we love best;　　.
For our Father, so kind, our lot has assigned
　In Utah, the queen of the west.

The bold mountains rise, and point to the skies,
　Like sentinels round our abode,
And vales calm and sweet repose at their feet —
　Fit home of the people of God.
From those cold, bleak forms, fit dwellings for storms,
　Flow the crystalline streams God has blest;
Rich harvests have smiled in the desert once wild,
　In Utah, the queen of the west.

The poor and oppressed, in this land of the west,
　Find plenty, and freedom, and joy;
Though the wicked may sneer, to us thou art dear,
　And fair as thine own sunny sky;
The Gospel's proclaimed to all here on earth,
　And the meek and the lowly rejoice;
From Babylon they flee to this land of the free —
　To Utah, the land of their choice.

Thy sisters first born, who tauntingly scorn,
　Shall joy to do honor to thee; ·
With each coming hour thy glory shall tower,
　Till the nations thy beauty shall see.

Thy triumph is nigh, oppression shall die,
  There is freedom within thee, and rest;
The years as they fleet shall bless our retreat,
  With peace in this land of the west.

YOUNG LOVE'S FIRST DREAM.

LAST night, mother, he told me so,
  As we walked by the pebbly stream,
And I woke so happy, so wild with joy,
  It seems like a fairy dream;
But his charming voice is ringing in my ear,
  As a dream voice could not be;
He's the best man you know in the wide, wide world,
  And he loves just only me.

Kiss me, mother, and share my joy,
  That has on my fortune smiled;
You have shared my sorrows, when'er I wept,
  Since I was a little child;
Do you chide me now? What could your darling do,
  When he plead with bended knee?
He's the best man you know in the wide, wide world,
  And he loves just only me.

Leave you, mother? It brings a pang
  To this light and bounding heart,
But if *he* were calling, the bride would go,
  Though you and the daughter part;
At a word from *him*, a beckon of his hand,
  I would cross the rolling sea;
He's the best man you know in the wide, wide world,
  And he loves just only me.

DIVORCED.

MONTHS of sunny life and fair,
Days that flitted — none knew where;
Hours of pleasure, hours of pain,
Hours that ne'er can come again;
They are gone, but do you find
You can leave them *all* behind?

Come not memories evermore
Drifting round you from that shore?
Words that lessened every care,
Thoughts no other e'er could share,
Duties that we ever met
With *one* thought, *can* you forget?

Can you calmly thus efface
From Life's tablet every trace
Of the hopes, and prayers, and tears,
We have shared in other years —
Can we all these memories smother
And "be nothing to each other?"

Can you break the golden chain
With its links of joy and pain?
Do you think it will decay
As the long years pass away?
That the bright strands e'er could fade
Tho' long hidden in the shade?

When for us life's task is o'er
And we tread its paths no more —
When 'mid shadows dimly falling,
We shall hear the angels calling,
As we calmly stand and wait,
Just outside the golden gate —

Then will these dark memories seem
But a phantom or a dream;
In that dawn of purer light
You will read all things aright;
False words will not seem as true
Till that morn — adieu, adieu!

THREE ANGELS.

THEY say this life is barren, drear and cold —
Ever the same sad song was sung of old —
Ever the same long weary tale is told;
And to our lips is held the cup of strife,
And yet — a little love can sweeten life.

They say our hands can grasp but joys destroyed,
Youth has but dreams, and age an aching void,
Which Dead Sea fruit long, long ago has cloyed;
Life is a night, with wild, cold tempests rife,
And yet — a little hope can brighten life.

They say we fling ourselves in wild despair,
Amidst the broken treasures scattered there —
Where all is wrecked, where all once promised fair,
And stab ourselves with sorrow's two-edged knife,
And yet — a little patience strengthens life.

Is it then true, this tale of woe and grief,
Of mortal anguish finding no relief?
Lo, midst the winter shines the laurel leaf —
Three angels share the lot of human strife —
Three angels glorify the path of life.

Love, Hope, and Patience cheer us on our way;
Love, Hope, and Patience form our spirit's stay;
Love, Hope, and Patience watch us day by day,
And bid the desert bloom with beauty vernal,
Until the earthly fades in the eternal.

NOVEMBER, 1871.

THE PIONEERS.

THEY were an exile band,
    Without a home to rest,
But, guided by a Father's hand,
    Their wand'rings have been blest.
Forsaken by their friends,
    Despised and scorned by foes,
They sought the aid the Highest sends,
    And in His strength arose.

O'er wide and lonely plains,
    Past dark Missouri's tide,
Our fathers sought a home, where they
    Might aye in peace abide;
Where each should have the right,
    In peace to worship God,
Uninfluenced by the pomp of pride,
    Unawed by tyrants' rod.

Amidst these mountains wild,
    O, can we e'er forget?
They made this desert land to bloom —
    The vales of Deseret.
Far from the scenes of vice
    Beyond their foe's domain,
They made this mountain land their choice,
    Let us their rights maintain.

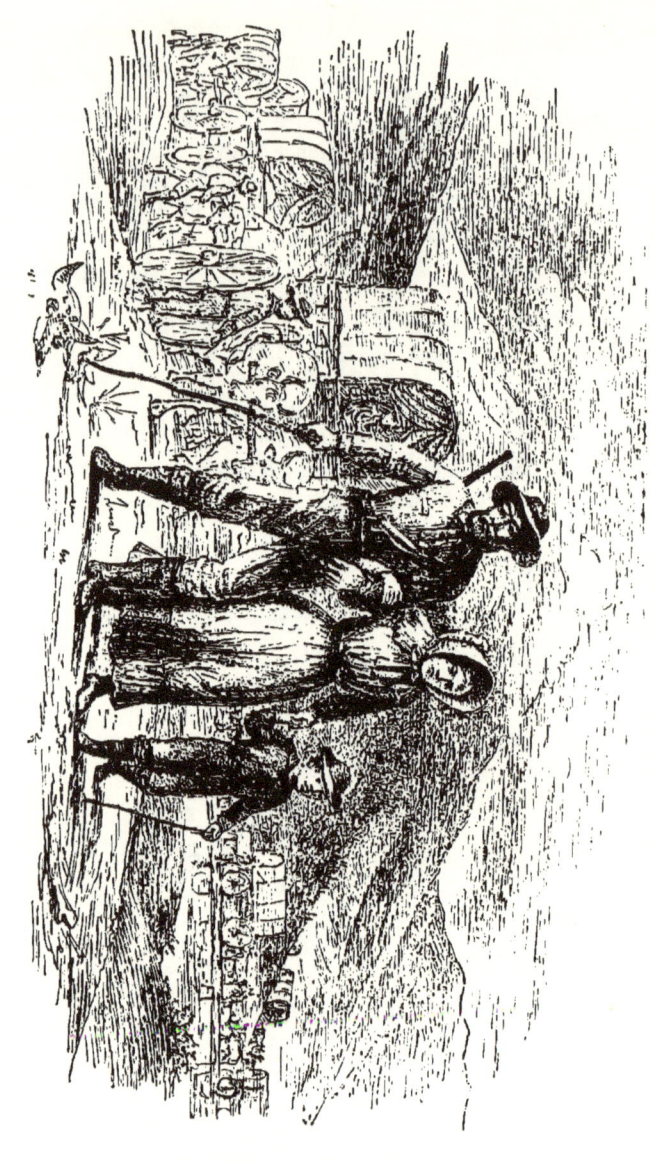

EARLY MEMORIES.

Read at a Reunion of Early Friends in 1880.

Good evening, friends, let us a moment ponder,
 And view again those scenes of youth most dear;
Let us again in childhood's bright days wander,
 And catch a memory that may bid us cheer.

Where are the bright scenes 'midst which once we'd linger,
 When life's harp seemed to sound but dulcet tones?
Ere age, with ruthless hand, had traced its finger
 Upon our brows? But, ah! those days are gone.

What though those sunny hours are not remaining,
 Still we will bless them for what they once were;
Nor can I say that life's deep joys are waning,
 Though in those pleasures I no more have share.

Some of those youths, the brave and noble-hearted,
 With whom we shared the sports of long ago,
Have anchor weighed, set sail, and hence departed
 To a far region, which we little know.

Still when we number sports of bygone moments,
 We'll reck their number as if they were here;
For still their memory clings around each romance
 Of early sorrow or of early cheer.

May we, like them, life's stormy voyage over,
 Rest in a land where joys perennial smile,
Trusting the promise of God's bright forever,
 To cheer the shadows of this little while.

8

A WIFE'S REMINISCENCE.

I REMEMBER my first valentine,
　　The cause of childish joy;
For I was then a tiny girl,
　　The sender but a boy.
It was indeed a gorgeous thing,
　　In brilliant colors wrought—
Above a bleeding, broken heart
　　Fat cupids fiercely fought.

The next love message I received
　　When I was sweet sixteen—
A pretty trifle, gilt with lace,
　　With tissue blue between;
Two pink hearts on an arrow fixed,
　　Surrounded by a wreath,
An altar, church, white doves and rings—
　　Hymeneal lines beneath.

The third—ah! friends, it was the last,
　　The dearest and the best;
It told a tale of honest love,
　　It brought me joy and rest;
A cream white shield of satin bore
　　A moss-rose wet with dew;
The name I loved was written on
　　A tiny scroll of blue.

The sender—well, I married him
　　One bright St. Valentine,
He spoke the words that made his name.
　　His home, his fortune mine.

I said 'twas the last valentine,
　　But that I now recall;
For I have still another one,
　　The sweetest of them all.

The sweetest and the prettiest,
　　A marvel 'tis of grace;
Pink, rounded limbs, pink, chubby feet,
　　And rosy, dimpled face,
Fourteenth of Febru'ry it came,
　　This baby-boy of mine;
What shall we call him, husband asks—
　　We'll call him Valentine.

THE WHITE STAIRWAY.

THE white sheet, woven in the clouds,
　　Enwraps the silent hills that lie,
Like giants, sleeping in their shrouds,
　　Clasped in the blue arms of the sky!

As the turf veils the peaceful dead,
　　Beneath this great white sheet of snow,
The winds tuck round their dreamless bed,
　　With hands unseen by us below!

Upon the mountain's furrowed brow,
　　By summer's awful thunder riven,
The winds are heaping banks of snow—
　　Building white stairways up to heaven!

THE TWO WORKERS.

Two workers in one field
    Toiled on from day to day;
Both had the same hard labor,
    Both had the same small pay.
With the same blue sky above,
    The same green grass below;
One soul was full of love,
    The other full of woe.

One leaped up with the light
    With the soaring of the lark;
One felt it ever night,
    For his soul was ever dark.
One heart was hard as stone,
    One heart was ever gay;
One worked with many a groan,
    One whistled all the day.

One had a flower-clad cot,
    Beside a merry mill;
Wife and children near the spot
    Made it sweeter, fairer still.
One a wretched hovel had,
    Full of discord, dirt, and din;
No wonder he seemed mad,
    Wife and children starved within.

Still they worked in the same field,
    Toiled on from day to day;
Both had the same hard labor,
    Both had the same small pay.

But they worked not with one will;
　　The reason let me tell:
Lo! the one drank at the still,
　　And the other at the well.

WHY WAS I LOOKING OUT?

RIGHT earnestly he sued my love,
　　For one kind look or smile;
I turned my face away from him,
　　And answered not a while;
Yet, as he crossed the little porch,
　　Perplexed by many a doubt,
He saw me through the jessamine —
　　Why was I looking out?

He pleaded for a little rose
　　That nestled in my hair;
I turned away in seeming scorn,
　　And left him lonely there;
Yet, as beneath my window-sill
　　He passed in dull despair,
He saw the rosebud in the grass —
　　How had it fallen there?

'Tis years ago; his sunny hair
　　Is still as brown and bright,
And on my hand a little ring
　　Is flashing in the light;
He is my own forevermore,
　　And he was mad to doubt,
Since first behind the jessamine
　　He caught me looking out.

TURNING GRAY.

LIFE's sands are running fast away,
  The buoyant step of youth has gone,
The falling hair is turning gray,
  And time seems now to hurry on
More fleetly than in days of yore—
  Before the heart became its prey:
Before 'twas saddened to the core—
  Before the hair was turning gray.

Yes, turning gray! age comes like snow,
  As still, and carves each careworn line;
Its wrinkles on the brow will grow;
  The hair with silvery streaks will shine;
The eyes their brightness lose, the hand
  Grow dry and tremulous and thin:
For life, alas! is quickly spanned,
  And death its gates soon closes in!

Ah, turning gray! we fain would hide,
  This sign how long with time we've been;
These deep'ning wrinkles side by side,
  Cut by the sorrows we have seen;
For feebler beats the heart as years
  More thickly cluster on our head;
As autumn raindrops hang like tears,
  On some fair flower that's nearly dead!

Like perished petals from the flower,
  Our hopes and wildest joys are laid:
Born only for a day or hour,
  Sweet gambols by the fancy played;

As age comes on we long for rest,
　As saints near shrines will long to pray;
But, ah! we loved that time the best,
　Before the hair was turning gray.

1878.

AN OLD ROAD.

A CURVE of green tree tops,
　And a common wall below,
And a winding road, that dips and drops,
　Ah me! where does it go?
Down to the lovely days
　Goes that familiar track,
And here I stand and wait and gaze,
　As if they could come back.

Somewhere beneath that hill
　Are children's running feet,
And a little garden fair and still,
　Were never flowers so sweet?
And a house within an open door,
　What was therein I know—
O! let me enter nevermore,
　But still believe it so.

Up this oft-trodden slope
　What visions rise and throng!
What keen remembrances of hope
　Lie shattered all along!
These flowers that never grew,
　Bloom they in any clime?
Can any spring to come renew
　What died in that sweet time?

Here I believed in fame,
    And found no room for fear;
Here sprang to meet what never came,
    Here loved—what is not here!
Not worth a moment's pause
    Seemed any fallen gem,
Not worth a sigh, a glance, because
    Life would be full of them.

The child in the fairy tale
    Dropped tokens as he passed,
So pierced the darksome forest veil
    And found his home at last;
I, in the falling day,
    Turn back through deeper gloom,
By gathered memories feel my way
    Only to find—a tomb.

For there they lie asleep,
    Eyes that made all things sweet,
Hands of true pressure, hearts more deep
    Than any left to beat;
A world where all was great,
    Paths trodden not, but seen:
Light streaming through an open gate—
    The world that might have been!

Pictures, and dreams, and tears—
    O Love, is this the whole?
Nay, wrap your everlasting years
    About my failing soul!
The lightest word you spake
    Beyond all time shall last—
These only sleep before they wake—
    In Love there is no Past!

THE MERCHANT.

Tare and tret, gross and net,
Box and hogshead, dry and wet:
Ready made, of every grade,
Wholesale, retail, will you trade?

Goods for sale, roll or bale,
Ell or quarter, yard or nail;
Every dye, will you buy?
None can sell as cheap as I!

Thus each day wears away,
And his hair is turning gray!
O'er his books he nightly looks,
Counts his gains and bolts his locks.

By and by he will die —
But the ledger book on high
Shall unfold how he sold,
How he got and used his gold!

St. Anthony, Minn., 1861.

LAZING.

Composed while shingling a roof on a hot day.

Give me a day, let business right itself,
Give me one day to drift in idleness
Along the shores of dreamland. Let me build
My castles in the air and dwell in them
A space, while yet the happy May-winds blow.

The oriole is come and in the thorn,
Among the greening buds, the cat-bird sings;
The fields are sweet, and in the sky is set
A tranquil glory. Let me go and lie
Upon the grass while happy May-winds blow.

I'd rather rest to-day than be a king,
For what are kings but slaves with golden chains?
Talk not of work, this is too sweet a day
To bow one's neck and tamely take the yoke
And I will not, while happy May-winds blow.

And if I fall asleep in Nature's arms,
Like weary child upon its mother's breast,
Let no one passing by awaken me,
For only once in all the rolling year
Comes holiday, while happy May winds blow.

MAY, 1872.

ISOLATION.

WE walk alone through all life's various ways,
Through light and darkness, sorrow, joy, and change;
And greeting each to each, through passing days,
　　　Still we are strange.

We hold our dear ones with a firm, strong grasp;
We hear their voices, look into their eyes;
And yet, betwixt us in that clinging clasp
　　　A distance lies.

We cannot *know their hearts*, howe'er we may
Mingle thought, aspiration, hope and prayer;
We cannot reach them, and in vain essay
　　　To enter there.

Still in each heart of hearts a hidden deep
Lies, never fathomed by its dearest, best;
With closest care our purest thoughts we keep,
And tenderest.

But, blessed thought! we shall not always so
In darkness and in sadness walk alone;
There comes a glorious day when we shall know
As we are known.

THE HILL DIFFICULTY.

"I beheld then that they all went on till they came to the foot of the hill Difficulty, at the bottom of which was a spring. . . . Christian now went to the spring (Isa. xlix. 10), and drank thereof to refresh himself," etc.—*Bunyan.*

THOU must go forward, pilgrim!
    Right up the hill;
The path is straight before thee,
    Right onward still.
By that ascent so rugged,
    Thy Lord has gone,
His people all must follow—
    Press boldly on!

Thou must go forward, pilgrim!
    Turn not aside;
Try not the tempting bye-ways
    Others have tried.
They have but strayed, and fallen
    To rise no more;
True danger lies behind thee
    Safety before!

Thou must go forward, pilgrim,
. Yet linger—stay
One moment at the fountain,
Here by the way.
The Master on his journey
Opened that spring,
Refreshment to the weary,
And strength to bring.

Hid in its depths of crystal
A mirror lies,
Where scenes of coming glory
May meet thine eyes.
Softly its murmuring waters
Repeat a tale
Of mercy ever flowing,
Never to fail.

Kneel by the brink so verdant,
Bathe thy hot brow;
Drink of the waters deeply—
Speed onward now!
Dread not the coming tempest,
The lion's roar;
Destruction is behind thee—
Heaven is before!

Thou must go forward, pilgrim,
O'er many a hill;
Yet shrink not from the prospect—
Press onward still!
Beside each mount of trial,
Each toil or pain,
The fountain of refreshment
Shall flow again.

CIVIL WAR.

Written after the battle of Mill Springs, and first published in the Shakopee Argus Wednesday, February 11, 1862.

"RIFLEMAN, shoot me a fancy shot
  Straight at the heart of yon prowling vedette;
Ring me a ball in the glittering spot
  That shines on his breast like an amulet."

"Ah, captain, here goes for a fine-drawn bead;
  There's music around when my barrel's in tune."
Crack! went the rifle, the messenger sped,
  And dead from his horse fell the ringing dragoon.

"Now, rifleman, steal through the bushes, and snatch
  From your victim some trinket to hansel first blood;
A button, or loop, or that luminous patch
  That gleams in the moon like a diamond stud."

"Oh, captain, I staggered, and sank on my track,
  When I gazed on the face of that fallen vedette,
For he looked so like you, as he lay on his back,
  That my heart rose upon me, and masters me yet.

"But I snatched off the trinket—this locket of gold;
  An inch from the centre my lead broke its way,
Scarce grazing the picture, so fair to behold,
  Of a beautiful lady in bridal array."

"Ha! rifleman, fling me the locket! 'Tis she,
  My brother's young bride—and the fallen dragoon
Was her husband. Hush, soldier, 'twas heaven's decree;
  We must bury him there by the light of the moon.

"But, hark! The far bugles their warnings unite;
· War is a virtue—weakness a sin;
There's a lurking and loping round us to-night—
Load again, rifleman, keep your hand in!"

NOT FIT TO BE KISSED.

"WHAT ails papa's mouf?" said a sweet little girl,
Her bright laugh revealing her teeth white as pearl;
"I love him and kiss him, and sit on his knee,
But the kisses don't smell good when he kisses me.

"Now, mamma"—her eyes op'ning wide as she spoke—
"Do you like nasty kisses of 'bacco and smoke?
They might do for boys, but for ladies and girls
I don't think them nice!" then she tossed her bright curls.

"Don't nobody's papa have a mouf nice and clean
With kisses like yours, mamma, that's what I mean?
I want to kiss papa, I love him so well;
But kisses don't taste good that have such a smell.

"It's nasty to smoke and eat 'bacco, and spit,
And the kisses ain't good and sweet, not a bit;"
And her innocent face wore a look of disgust
As she gave out her verdict, so earnest and just.

Yes, yes, little darling! your wisdom has seen
That kisses for daughters and wives should be clean;
For kisses lose something of nectar and bliss
From mouths that are stained and unfit for a kiss.

OCTOBER, 1864.

DRIFTING.

We meet as we have always met,
　　And part as kindly as before;
We speak in tender tones, and yet
　　We know that love is there no more.

There was a time, in days gone by,
　　We truly loved without deceit;
My love was all I had, and I
　　Laid down the trifle at your feet.

I gave you all, and in return
　　You gave to me a fresh young heart;
But time that changes all is stern,
　　And we have drifted far apart.

We know that constant dropping tears
　　Will wear away the hardest stone,
And that an endless tide of years
　　Will leave the firmest chains undone.

Thus disappointments, one by one,
　　Will blight the life, and hope departs:
And thus has time at length undone
　　The silken cord that bound our hearts.

Farewell, for we must part at last,
　　And if we ever love again,
I trust this lesson of the past
　　Will help us to be faithful then.

SPEAK THY THOUGHT.

If a truth has shone within thee,
　　Is it manly, just, or brave —
Captive of the world's opinion —
　　To conceal the light it gave?

All conviction should be valiant,
　　Tell thy truth — if truth it be —
Never seek to stem its current,
　　Thoughts like rivers find the sea.

Speak thy thought, if thou believ'st it,
　　Let it jostle whom it may,
Every seed that grows to-morrow,
　　Lies beneath a clod to-day.

If our sires, the noble-hearted
　　Pioneers of things to come,
Had like thee been weak and timid,
　　Traitors to themselves, and dumb,

Where would be our free opinion —
　　Where the right to speak at all,
If our sires, like thee, mistrustful,
　　Had been deaf to duty's call?

Where would be triumphant science,
　　Searching with her fearless eyes,
Through the infinite creation,
　　For the soul that underlies.

Where would be those inspirations,
    Launched 'midst apathy and scorn?
How could noontide ever greet us,
    But for dawning of the morn?

Though an honest thought, outspoken,
    Lead thee into chains or death —
What is life compared with virtue,
    Shalt thou not survive thy breath?

Have not ages long departed,
    Groaned and toiled and bled for thee,
If the Past has lent thee wisdom,
    Pay it to Futurity.

JUNE, 1878.

MY NATIVE LAND.

Hurrah! hurrah! my native land,
    Upon our bows at last,
The glistening tears around my heart,
    Their evening rainbow cast.
Give back your foam, ye kindly waves,
    And speed my vessel free,
Old native hills, I'm coming now,
    A wanderer home to thee.

Be still, be still, my throbbing heart,
    Go back ye childish tears:
But oh, I've waited for this hour,
    Through many weary years.
I've toiled beneath a burning sun,
    And slept upon the plain,
That I might once more plant my foot —
    On native soil again.

The same, the same, I know it well,
    It rises on the gale,
The sweet old scent of clover bloom,
    From every flowery vale.
I feel, ah me, as if my heart,
    Had never been away,
And long-dried springs of early joy,
    Flow full as in life's May.

Ye smile! ye smile! to welcome me,
    Tho' twenty years are by,
Since from my eyes ye stole a tear,
    And from by breast a sigh.
My locks were dark and glossy then,
    Though now they're thin and gray;
But love of home grows riper, aye,
    When summer dies away.

The years! the years! have passed me o'er,
    And changes I have seen;
Perhaps the folks that knew me then,
    Will not be as they've been.
Perchance the maidens that I loved,
    Will wonder whence I came,
And playmates of my early days
    Unheeding ask my name.

Ah well! ah well! old native hills,
    I see no change in you,
The blue lake's foam is still as white,
    The pine-clad hills as blue.
I'll live my early life again,
    Amid your forests old;
Though eyes have lost their glance of love,
    And human hearts grow cold.

Hurrah! hurrah! my native land.
　Thy pine-clad hills at last,
The tears are starting to my eye,
　My heart is beating fast.
Give back, ye kindly waves, give back,
　And speed my vessel free;
Old native hills, I'm coming now, ·
　A wanderer home to thee.

APRIL, 1880.

CHILDREN AT THEIR PLAY.

I've listened at the early dawn
　The lark salute the morn,
The robin and the linnet's note
　Poured from the blooming thorn;
I've heard, at evening's dewy close,
　The blackbird's melting lay,
But there's no music half so sweet
　As children at their play.

I've heard unrivalled Patti sing
　Columbia's glorious strains,
And lend even poesy a grace
　Beyond the poet's pains;
Parepa Rosa's marvelous voice
　Hath borne my soul away,
But there's no music half so sweet
　As children at their play.

I've sat within enchantment's spell,
　And lost to meaner things,
While Paganini's master hand,
　With magic touched the strings;

But there's no sweet-toned instrument,
  Which cunning hands essay.
Can yield a music to my heart
  Like children at their play.

All nature teems with holiest sounds,
  On listening ears they fall—
Ye rivers, streams, ye lands, ye waves,
  There's music in you all ;
But see the school-boys just let loose,
  Exulting bound away—
Then who can tell of music sweet
  As children at their play?

WE'VE DRUNK FROM THE SAME CANTEEN.

To my friend and comrade, William Brokensha.

THERE are bonds of all sorts in this world of ours—
Fetters of friendship and ties of flowers—
  And true lover's knots, I ween.
The boy and the girl are bound by a kiss,
But there's never a bond, old friend, like this—
  We have drunk from the same canteen.

It was sometimes water, and sometimes milk,
Sometimes apple-jack, fine as silk ;
  But whatever the tipple has been,
We shared it together in bane or bliss,
And I warm to you, friend, when I think of this—
  We have drunk from the same canteen.

The rich and great sit down to dine,
And quaff to each other in sparkling wine,
    From glasses of chrystal and green —
But I guess in their golden potations they miss
The warmth of regard to be found in this —
    We have drunk from the same canteen.

We've shared our blankets and tent together,
And marched and fought in all kinds of weather,
    And hungry and full we've been ;
Had days of battle and days of rest,
But this memory I cling to and love the best —
    We have drunk from the same canteen.

For when wounded I lay on the outer slope,
With my blood flowing fast and but little hope
    On which my faint spirit might lean,
Oh! then, I remember, you crawled to my side,
And, bleeding so fast, it seemed both must have died —
    Yes, we drank from the same canteen.

WHO WAS HE?

The following was written in a soldiers' hospital, not long after the battle of
Stone River, and first published in the *Shakopee Argus*, Wednesday, February 18th,
1863. It is here given as originally published.

INTO a ward of the canvas hall,
    Where the wounded and dying lay —
Wounded by shell, or bayonet, or ball,
    Somebody's darling was borne one day;
He who was gallant, and daring, and brave,
    Yet bearing on his pale sweet face,
(Soon to be hid by the dust of the grave),
    The lingering light of his boyhood's grace.

Matted and clotted the locks of gold,
    That once lay smooth on that fair young brow;
Mute are those lips with a tale untold,
    For somebody's darling is dying now;
Smooth from his beautiful manly brow   ·
    Back that straying lock of gold,
Fold his hands on his bosom now —
    They are already growing cold.

Kiss him once for somebody's sake,
    Breathe a prayer, though soft and low;
A tiny lock from his temples take —
    No fairer prize for a mother, you know;
Haply her hand hath rested there,
    Or was it a sister's, soft and white?
Did they stroke those locks — the saddened pair —
    When he marched away in the morning light?

God only knows, he was somebody's love —
    To somebody he was the joy and pride;
Somebody wafted his name above,
    Night and morning and even tide.
Somebody wept when he marched away,
    Looking so handsome, hopeful and grand;
Somebody's kiss on his forehead lay,
    Somebody clung to his parting hand.

Someone at home is waiting for him,
    Yearning to hold him again to her heart;
But there he lies, with his bright eyes dim,
    And the smiling childlike lips apart;
Tenderly bury the fair young dead,
    Unknown though it be the name he should bear,
Yet carve on the rude slab at his head,
    SOMEONE'S DARLING REPOSES HERE.

Mute are those lips with a tale untold,
For somebody's darling is dying now.

THE MOUNTAIN BOY.

BENEATH my feet the valleys lie,
A mountain shepherd boy am I;
The sunbeams bright, here first I see—
They tarry longest here with me,
 For I'm the mountain boy.
 The mountain boy, the mountain boy,
 For I'm the mountain boy.

Here is the fountain's secret home,
My drink comes fresh from rock and foam—
It springs o'er rocks in wild career,
Its sound is music to my ear,
 For I'm the mountain boy, etc.

The mountain truly is my own,
The storms may rage and weirdly moan,
And sweep from north to south along,
O'er all still rings my cheerful song,
 I am the mountain boy, etc.

When thunders roll and lightnings flash,
I stand above the stormy crash;
What care I for the storm-king's glance,
Above me spreads the blue expanse,
 For I'm the mountain boy, etc.

And should Columbia call to arms,
Should foemen fierce spread dire alarms;
Then we'll descend and join the throng,
And wield our swords, and sing our song,
 For we're the mountain boys, etc.

TOWARD SUNSET.

THE sun of life has passed its noon,
 The shadows stretch away,
And, deepening into denser gloom,
 Foretell the close of day.
Weary and fainting where we stand
We reach to grasp our Father's hand.

One after one the fleeting hours
 Have banished life's bright schemes;
The springtide joys that once were ours,
 The summer noon-day dreams,
How soon, alas, they pass from sight,
And leave us but a winter night.

But not entirely cold and sad
 The days of years now flown:
Full many a morn and evening had
 A brightness of their own.
Content looks forward full of cheer
To all that may await us here.

There is a land where night or cloud
 No sombre shadows fling,
Where wailing blasts and tempests loud
 No solemn requiem sing;
But all is calm, serene and fair;
Eternal noon-day reigneth there.

There is a land, and oh, how blest,
 The souls forever free,
Who wander 'mid its vales, or rest

Beneath Life's spreading tree:
And dread no parting grief to share,
But dwell in love together there.

In nature's course 'tis yours and mine,
    Ere long to tread that shore:
To join, beyond the realm of time,
    Those who have gone before:
Who wait upon the golden strand,
And beckon us with outstretched hand.

THE BACHELOR'S CONFESSION.

OH! my bachelor-life is jolly and free;
No curtain-lectures to harass the "wee
Sma' hours;" no babies around my knee;
Nobody to scold about the night key,
Or to open my letters, or cry to see
The bill (?) that my tailor (?) marked "Private" to me.

The wine that I sip is sweet—ah! sweet;
And every hour, with joy replete,
Maketh a perfect whole, complete;
Morning, and noontide, and evening greet
With laughter, and speed with flying feet—
Each a rose-crowned god, a Mercury fleet.

I never shall marry: Why should I? Why
Should I shackle my life, and madly fly
Into a knot I can never untie?
Why cloud the sun in the summer-sky?
I might as well give up the ghost and die
As to marry. Why should I—I?

No! I'm not a cynic, or bitter, or cold;
I love each thread of the waving gold
That falls with crinkle, and curl, and fold,
Over your shoulders of faultless mold;
Your eyes that are blue as the heavens old,
Oft stir my heart with a thrill untold.

But I love a dozen besides. I fell
Into the habit when young, my belle;
And, if I were a benedict, I'd rebel,
Or forget, and love my neighbor so well
That Grundy the story would swiftly tell,
The scan. mag. page of the *Times* to swell.

No heart? Oh! there's where the mischief lies;
The troublesome thing will leap and rise
Into my throat when starry eyes
(Angels I'am sure, in human guise,)
Look into mine with a sweet surprise,
As if they had just strayed out of the skies.

Still, I never shall marry. You call me a "Bear,"
A "Heathen," "Blase," and say "You don't care;
You'd pity my wife if one fell in a snare
I set to trap her." I pray you forbear;
Don't say what you know isn't true or fair,
Without rhyme or reason, neither here nor there.

And don't repeat that you wouldn't have me!
It may not be gallant, but there we agree;
You're a flirt; I'm a "Bear;" so don't you see
A more wretched union could never be?
Ere the honeymoon waned I should pine to be free,
Like a Neptune chained far away from the sea.

"Been happier?" Bother, don't trouble me, pet,
To think about things I should like to forget.
I have friends and money, and never fret;
I am jolly, and free; and yet—and yet—
Pshaw! why waste time in a useless regret?
Though life is not bliss 'twere folly to fret,
Or mourn o'er the past for what fate would not let.

TRANSLATIONS FROM VARIOUS AUTHORS.

-

THE LAND OF REST.

(FROM THE GERMAN OF UHLAND).

THERE is a land where beauty will not fade,
  Nor sorrow dim the eye;
Where true hearts will not sink nor be dismayed,
  And love will never die.
Tell me, I fain would go,
For I am burdened with a heavy woe;
The beautiful have left me all alone;
The true, the tender, from my gaze have gone,
And I am weak and fainting with despair;
Where is it? Tell me where?

Friend, thou must trust to Him who trod before
  The lonely path of life;
Must bear in meekness, as He meekly bore,
  Sorrow, and toil, and strife.
Think how the Son of God
These thorny paths has trod;
Think how He longed to go,
Yet tarried out for thee, the appointed woe.

Think of his loneliness in places dim,
When no man comforted nor cared for Him;
Think how He prayed, unaided and alone,
In that dread agony, "Thy will be done!"
Friend do not then despair,
Christ, in his heaven of heavens, will hear thy prayer.

ETERNITY.

(TRANSLATED FROM THE GERMAN).

ETERNITY! Eternity!
How long art thou eternity?
Yet swiftly time sweeps on to thee—
Swift as the steed to victory,
The flying post, the speeding bark,
The arrow hasting to the mark.

Eternity! Eternity!
How long art thou, eternity?
As on a sphere no eye may scan,
Or where it ends, or where began;
Eternity! within thy round,
Nor spring nor issue can be found.

Eternity! Eternity!
How long art thou, eternity?
Within a circle hidest thou,
Whose centre is a constant *now*,
Whose circuit as a perpetual *never*,
Receding ever and for ever.

Eternity! Eternity!
How long art thou, eternity?
A swallow might be tasked to drain
The world's huge substance, hill and plain,
Each thousand years a single grain;
Yet wouldst thou then, as now, remain.

Eternity! Eternity!
How long art thou, eternity?
The ocean's sands and drops we count

The fraction of a whole amount;
The mighty cycles of thine age,
No calculus could ever guage.

Eternity! Eternity!
How long art thou, eternity?
Mortal! as long as God shall be,
So long shall my swift current flow,
So shall thine endless being be
For thou shalt live and thou shalt know.

EARTH'S TRIBUTE.

The poet, Arthur Mueller, one of the editors of *The Gartenlaube*, committed
suicide at Munich. A few hours before his death he wrote the poem, the translation
of which is given below:

O, EARTH, my mother — take again thy son
From all this wretched, narrow littleness,
This low, abhorrent creeping pitifulness.
Mother of all, would that my race were run!

All powerfully I am drawn out and up,
My soul would mingle with eternity,
And for a breath of perfect purity,
Down to the dregs have I now drained life's cup.

My work is now complete. For I have tried, in sooth
Struggled and suffered for liberty and truth.
What besides wounds this life has left at length,
Is but a vapid shadow of my former strength.

Let me in silence sleep upon thy breast —
O, earth, my mother! Give thy tired son rest —
Silently rest; and be a part of you,
Mother, thou knowest that it is my due.

HOLD STILL.

PAIN's furnace-heat within me quivers,
  God's breath upon the flames doth blow,
And all my heart in anguish shivers,
  And trembles at the fiery glow,
And yet I whisper: As God will!
And, in His hottest fire, hold still.

He comes and lays my heart all heated
  On the hard anvil, minded so
Into His own fair shape to beat it,
  With His great hammer, blow on blow
And yet I whisper: As God will!
And, at His heaviest blows, hold still.

He takes my softened heart, and beats it,
  The sparks fly off at every blow.
He turns it o'er and o'er and heats it,
  And lets it cool and makes it glow.
And yet I whisper: As God will!
And in His mighty hand hold still.

Why should I murmur? For the sorrow
  Thus only longer-lived would be.
Its end may come, and will to-morrow,
  When God has done his work in me.
So I say, trusting: As God will!
And, trusting to the end, hold still.

He kindles for my profit, purely
  Affliction's glowing, fiery brand,
And all His heaviest blows are surely
  Inflicted by a Master-hand;
So I say, praying: As God will!
And, hoping in His love, hold still.

10

TROSTEWORTE AN CHRISTLICHE ELTERN BEIM FRUHER VERLUFT IHRER KINDER.

(DR. KARL VICTOR RITTERMANN.)

SIE sind gestorben aber nicht verloren,
Die Kleinen deren Tod ihr früh beweint!
Der Herr hat sie zu Pflantzen sich erkoren,
Zu blüken wo die ewige Sonne scheint.

Schaut nicht zurück, blickt hoher als auf Grüfte —
Die Gruft, sie birgt mer moderndes Gebein,
Den Geist umweh'n des Paradieses düfte
In Gottes Garten frühlingsmild und rein.

Sind bitter auch der frühen Trennung Schmertzen
Sind sie doch kurtz und blos der Leib getrennt,
Die Liebe einigt trotz dem Grab die Hertzen,
Die Liebe welche keinen Wechsel kennt.

Schon winkt nach Tod und düsterm Trennungsgrauen
Des Wiedersehens freundlich Morgenroth,
Schon tagt der Glaube über Frühlingsauen
Und webt der Hoffnung Schleier über Grab und Tod.

Ist auch des Kindes Plätzchen in dem Hause
Der Sonntagschule und der Kirche leer.
Ist's doch entrückt der Erde Sturmgebrause
Singt seine "Jubeltone" dort am gläsern Meer.

Es kniet nicht mehr der Mutter still zur Zeite·
Und lalt mit frommem Sinne sein Gebet,
Doch betet's in Verklarung voller Freude
Wo man nur dankt, nicht mehr als Sünder fleht.

COMFORTING WORDS TO THOSE WHO HAVE LOST THEIR CHILDREN.

(TRANSLATED FROM RITTERMANN.)

They have passed hence, but they're not lost forever,
    Those little ones whose fate ye early mourn —
Those flowers, the Master for Himself hath gathered
    To bloom eternal, and e'en heaven adorn.

Call them not back, look higher than the grave —
    The grave but holds their moldering remains —
Their spirits now, by heavenly breezes fanned,
    Dwell in the land where spring eternal reigns.

'Twas bitter, sad, the smart of early parting,
    'Tis only short, and unto mortals strange;
Love still unites, in spite of death and sorrow —
    Eternal love, which knows no time or change.

Already gleams 'yond death's dark separation,
    The resurrection morning's spring-like breath —
E'en now Faith wafts us over blooming fields —
    Hope weaves assurance over grave and death.

The children now no more in wonted places
    Are found at school, or where they used to roam,
While still we hear the rustling of death's tempest —
    They sing triumphant in their spirit home.

They kneel no more by mother's knee so quiet,
    And lisp with pious voice the children's prayer —
Now prayer is changed to praise, and grief to gladness
    Where saints but thank, not plead, as sinners there.

Es wartet auch im Engelchor der kleinen
Wohl an des Paradieses goldenem Thor,
Bis seine lieben Eltern dort erscheinen
Und führt sie jubelnd zu dem Strahlenlhron empor.

Ein kind im Himmel — heiliger Gedanke!
.Ein kind im Himmel — himlicher Magnet!
Er zieht den Geist durch Welt und ihre Schranke,
Bis er im Wiederseh'n vor Gottes Throne steht.

TREUE UND REDLICHKEIT.

Ueb immer Treue und Redlichkeit
    Bis an dein kühles Grab,
Und weiche keinen Finger breit,
    Von Gottes wegen ab.

Dann wirst du wie auf grünen Auen,
    Durchs Pilgerleben geh'n;
Dann Kannst du ohne Furcht und Grau'n
    Dem Tod' ins Auge seh'n.

Dann wird die Sichel und der Pflug
    Dir in der Haud se leicht;
Dann singest du beim Wasserkrug,
    Als war dir wein gereicht.

Dann segnen Eukel deine Gruft
    Und weinen Thräneu drauf,
Und Sommerblumen voller duft
    Blüh'n ans deu Thränen auf.

They're waiting there in angel choir, the loved ones,
　　Close on to Paradise's golden door—
Till parents loved, in triumph there appearing,
　　Then lead them joyful o'er the starry floor.

A child in heaven! O, the holy thought!
　　A child in heaven! O, attractive wand!
It draws the spirit from life's care and sorrow,
　　Till from death's waking at heaven's gate we stand.

FIDELITY AND HONESTY.

Live ever true and honestly,
　　Even to the dark cold grave,
And never swerve a finger breadth
　　From laws the Savior gave.

Then whilst thou, as on meadows green,
　　Thy life's short journey go,
Then canst thou look death in the face,
　　Nor fear or trembling know.

Then will the sickle and the plow,
　　Seem light in hands of thine;
Then wilst thou sing at water-flask,
　　As though they gave thee wine.

Then children's children on thy grave
　　Shall weep with happy tears,
And out those tears sweet summer flowers
　　Shall bloom in after years.

DER TAUCHER.

(A GERMAN LEGEND).

WER wagt es Rittersmann oder Knapp,
    Zu tauchen in diesen Schlund,
Einen goldnen Becher werf ich hinab,
    Verschlungen schon hat in der schwartze Mund,
Wer mir den Becher kann wieder zeigen,
Er mag ihn behatten, er ist sein eigen.

Der Konig spricht es und wirft von der Höh,
    Der Klippe, die schroff und steil,—
Hinaushangt in die unendliche See
    Den Becher in der Charybde Geheul,
Wer ist der Behertze, ich frage wieder
Zu tauchen in diese Tiefe neider.

Und die Ritter, die Knappen um ihn her,
    Vernehmen's und schweigen still,
Sehen hinab im wilde Meer,
    Und keiner den Becher gewinnen will,
Und der Konig zum dritten mal wieder fraget,
"Ist Keiner der sich hinunter waget."

Doch Alles noch stumm bleibt wie zuvor,
    Und ein Edelknecht sanft und keck,
Tritt aus der Knappen zagendem Chor,
    Und den Gürtel wirft den Mantel weg,
Und alle die Manner umher und Frauen
Auf den herlichen Jüngling verwundert schanen.

Und wie er tritt des Felsen Hang,
    Und blickt in den Schlund hinab,
Die Wasser die sie hinunter schlang,

A LEGEND OF THE MAELSTROM.

(TRANSLATED FROM SCHILLER).

Who will venture of all ye noblemen bold,
    To dive in this whirling abyss?
I throw in the maelstrom this goblet of gold —
    'Tis already engulfed, the dark waters hiss;
Whoever that cup from the depths shall regain,
His prize it shall be evermore to retain.

The king while thus speaking the goblet had flung
    To the depths 'neath the cliff's rugged steep,
Which o'er the dark waves of the wild torrent hung;
    "Who dares for the goblet go down in the deep?
Who is the brave-hearted, come hither to me
Who dares to dive down to the depths of the sea."

The noblemen stand there, nor venture a motion,
    They all hear it but no one replies,
They silently gaze on the dark depths of ocean —
    None wish to attempt the bold deed for the prize;
Then arose the king's voice o'er the whirlpool's weird sound,
And three times repeated, "Can no one be found?"

In silence they stood, by the monarch's words cowed,
    Till a youth, gentle, noble and brave,
Stepped fearlessly out from the tremulous crowd
    And prepared for a plunge in the wave;
The lords and the ladies are lost in amaze,
And silently at the youth wonderingly gaze.

As he stepped to the brink, it hisses and lashes
    Like water which quenches a brand;
High up the dampening spray surges and splashes,

Die Charybde jetzt brullend wiedergab,
Und wie mit des fernen Donners Getose,
Enstürtzen sie schaümend dem finstern Schoose.

Doch endlich da legt sich die wilde Gewalt,
    Und schwartz ans dem weissen Schaum
Klafft hinunter ein gahnender Spalt,
    Grundlos, als ging's in den Hollenraum,
Und reissend sieht man die brandenden Wogen,
Hinab in strudelnden Trichter gezogen.

Jelzt schnell ch'die Brandung wiederkehrt,
    Der Jungling sich zu Gott befiehlt,
Und —ein Schrei des Entsetzens wird rings gehort,
    Und schon hat ihn der Wirbel hinweggespult,
Und geheimnissvoll uber dem kühnen Schwimmer
Schliesst sich der Rachen; er zeigt sich nimmer.

Wohl manches Fahtzeug vom Strudel gefasst,
    Schoss gäh in die Tiefe hinab,
Doch zerschmettert nur rangen sich Kiel und Mast,
    Hervor aus dem Alles verschlingenden Grab,
Und heller und heller wie Sturmes Sausen,
Hört man's näher und immer näher brausen.

    *   *   *   *   *   *   *

Und sieh! ans dem finstern flutenden Schoos,
    Da habet sich's schwanen weiss,
Und ein Arm und ein glanzender Nacken wird bloss,
    Und es rudert mit Kraft und mit emsigem Fleiss,
Und er ist's und hoch in seiner Linken
Schwinkt er den Becher mit freudigem Winken.

Und athmete lang und athmete tief,
    Und begruste das himmlische Licht,
Mit Frohlocken es einer dem Andern rief;

Floating on the wild waves of that dark heaving tomb,
What see ye like swan neck so white?
'Tis the arm of the diver who peers from the gloom,
And floats on the waves in their eddying flight.

And flood after flood rolls on without end —
Endless, exhausted, with roar like far thunder,
Filling beholders with terror and wonder.

But seeming at length, the mad, wild billows cease,
    And, black 'midst the foaming white spray,
Wide opens a fathomless, gloomy abyss,
    As if to hell's regions of darkness the way;
Swiftly onward the furious breakers are borne,
Or down in the depths of the vortex are drawn.

Now, quick, while a moment the breakers more still,
    To heaven he confideth his soul;
A plunge — a wild cry of horror, so shrill —
    And o'er him the whirlpool's wild surging waves roll —
The jaws of the water-cave over him close,
And but to the diver its secrets disclose.

"Farewell, gallant youth," cried the king "thou art brave,
    From our sight thou art evermore past,
For many the proud bark that sails o'er the wave
    The vortex resistless has torn keel from mast.
What those howling depths dark in their bosom conceal,
No living soul ever to us will reveal."

    *   *   *   *   *   *   *

Floating on the wild waves of that dark-heaving tomb,
    What see ye like swan neck so white?
'Tis the arm of the diver who peers from the gloom,
    And floats on the waves in their eddying flight,
It is he, with what joy, he raises his hand,
And waves the gold goblet to those on the strand.

Exhausted he lay, breaths long and deep drew,
    When returned to the sun's lovely light,
The courtiers with joy shout to each as they view:

"Er lebt! er ist da! es behielt ihn nicht,
Aus dem Grab aus den strudelnden Wasserhohle,
Hat der Brave gerettet die lebende Seele."

Und er kommt, es umringt ihn die jubelnde Schaar;
    Zu des Königs Füssen er sinkt,
Den Becher reicht er ihm kniend dar,
    Und der König der lieblichen Tochter winkt,
Die füllt ihn mit funkelndem Wein bis zum Rande,
Und der Jüngling sich also zum König wandte.

Lang lebe der König! Es freue sich,
    Wer da athmet im rosigten Licht!
Da unten aber ist's fürchterlich,
    Und der Mensch versuche die Götter nicht,
Und begehre nimmer und nimmer zu schauen,
Was sie gnädig bedecken mit Nacht und Grauen.

Es riss mich hinunter blitzesschnell,
    Da stürtzt mir aus felsigtem Schacht,
Wild flutend entgegen ein reissender Quell,
    Mich packt des Doppelstroms wuthende Macht,
Und wie einen Kreisel mit schwindelndem Drehen,
Trieb mich's um, ich konnte nicht wiederstehen.

Den unter mir lag's noch bergetief,
    In purpurner Finsterniss da,
Und obs hier dem Ohre gleich ewig schlief,
    Das Auge mit Schaudern hinunter sat,
Und dräuend wies mir die grimmigen Zähne,
Der entsetzliche Hay, des Meeres Hyäne.

Und da hing ich und war's mir mit Gruusen bewusst,
    Von der menschlichen Hülfe so weit,
Unter Larven die einzige fuhlende Brust,

"He is living. he comes, from the regions of night,
He has vanquished the foe, and from out the dark wave
Comes the living soul saved by the hand of the brave."

Rejoice! around him they gather in glee,
　　Who has rescued the prize from the ocean;
At the king's feet he offers the cup on bent knee,
　　The king cries, "Bring wine," to his daughter makes motion:
The lovely maid fills it with wine to the brim,
To the king turned the youth, and thus addressed him—

"Long life to the king, may he happy e'er be,
　　And breathe in the glad sunny ray,
For fearful it is in the depths of the sea;
　　In the secrets of God let mortal ne'er pry,
Or dare evermore to bring to the light
What His mercy has hidden 'neath terror and night.

"With tempestuous speed as it tore me along,
　　What torrents from dark caverns gushed;
A billowy flood so resistless and strong,
　　That it seized me and tossed me, as o'er me it rushed.
Like a pebble it hurled me, for vain is the dream,
Of mortal contending 'gainst the might of that stream.

"Far beneath me the sea as a mountain was deep,
　　In darkness and silence it rolled;
There monsters were swarming in fearful array,
　　With a shudder of horror the eye could behold,
And menacing gleamed the white teeth in the dark
Of the ocean's hyena, the terrible shark.

"By horrors oppressed to the great God I cried,
　　There far from humanity's aid,
And there on a cliff jutting out at my side,

Allein in der grässlichen Einsamkeit,
Tief unter dem Schall der menschlichen Rede,
Bei den Ungeheuern der traurigen Ode.

Und schaudernd dacht' ich's da kroch's heran,
    Regte hundert Gelenke zugleich,
Will schnappen nach mir in des Shrecken's Wahn,
    Lass ich los der Koralle umklamerten Zweig,
Gleich fasst mich der Strudel mit rasendem Toben,
Doch es war mir zum Heil, er riss mich Oben."

Der König darob sich verwundert schier,
    . Und spricht "der Becher ist dein,
Und diesen Ring noch bestimm' ich dir,
    Geschmückt mit dem köstlichsten Edelstein,
Versuchst du's noch einmal und bringst mir Kunde,
Was du sahst auf des Meeres tiefunterstein Grunde.

Das hörte die Tochter mit weichem Gefuhl,
    Und mit schmeichelndem Munde sie fleht;
, "Lass, Vater, genug sein das grausame Spiel!
    Er hat euch bestanden, was Keiner besteht,
Und könnt ihr des Hertzens Gelusten nicht zähmen,
So mögen die Ritter den Knappen beschamen."

Drauf der König greift nach dem Becher schnell,
    In den Strudel ihn schleudert hinein,
Und schaffst du den Becher mir wieder zur Stell,
    So sollst du der trefflichste Ritter mir sein,
Und sollst sie als Ehgemahl heut' noch umarmen,
Die jetzt für dich bittet mit zartem erbarmen."

Da ergrieft's ihm die Seele mit Himmelsgewalt,
    Und es blitzt aus den Augen ihm kühn,
Und er sieht errothen die schöne Gestalt,

Surrounded by corals the goblet was laid;
Deep, deep where the accents of man never rung,
To a cliff 'midst the monsters of ocean I hung.

"'Mid demons, the only one sensitive breast,
    I shuddered, for lo! the monsters crept near —
Those hideous forms which those regions infest
    Drew near me — in the madness of fear,
I let go the cliff for the horrors before me,
O thanks! the furious current up bore me."

At this tale wonderment shadowed the king,
    And he cried, "Brave youth, the goblet is thine;
Bold swimmer still more, I will give thee this ring,
    'Tis set with rare gems as e'er came from the mine,
If once more thou wilt dive, bring word unto me,
What exists farther down on the floor of the sea."

As the daughter' heard this she was filled with emotion,
    Love and pity caressingly plead,
"Cease, father this cruel sport with the ocean;
    The youth is proved brave, by his perilous deed,
If thou wilst not abandon thy heart's wild desire,
Let these knights endeavor to shame the brave squire."

But the king seized the goblet and quickly again
    Hurled it down in the furious sea,
"Noble youth, if thou bringest the goblet thus thrown,
    My first, and my brave peerless knight shalt thou be.
And my daughter to-day thou shalt have for thy bride,
Who pleads for thee meekly with tears at my side."

Then a might seized his soul that was terrible now,
    And a strange light flashed forth from his eyes;
He sees the red blush on that beautiful brow.

Und sieht sie erbleichen und sinken hin,
Da treibts' ihn köstlichen Preis zu erwerben,
Und sturtzt hinunter auf Leben und Sterben.

Whol hort man die Brandung, whol kehrt sie zurick,
    Sie verkundigt der donnernde Schall;
Da buckt sich hinunter mit liebendem Blick,
    Es kommen, es kommen die Wasser all,
Sie rauschen herauf, sie rauschen nieder,
Den Jungling bringt kines wieder.

MIGNON.

AUSZUG VON "WILHELM MEISTER" EINER DER SCHONSTE WERKE VON GOTHE).

Kennst du das Land wo die Citronen blühn,
Im dunkeln Laub die Gold-Orangen glühn,
Ein saufter Wind vom blauen Himmel weht,
Die Myrthe still und hoch der Lorbeer steht.
    Kennst du es wohl?
        Dahin! Dahin!
Möcht' ich mit dir, O mein Geliebter ziehn.

Kennst du das Haus? Auf Säulen ruht sein Dach,
Es glänzt der Saal, es schimmert das Gemach,
Und Marmorbilder stehn und sehn mich an;
Was hat man dir, du armes Kind gethan?
    Kennest du es wohl?
        Dahin! Dahin!
Möcht' ich mit dir, O mein Beschützer, ziehn,

Convulsive she sobs—to win the loved prize,
To win, or to perish, by hope hurried on,
For life, or for death—a plunge—he is gone.

The wild waters roll, the billows still break,
    And resound on the pebbly shore,
O'er the foam-crested waves lovers lingering look
    The vortex rolls on as before;
Currents rush to the surface then downwards they sweep,
But the youth never comes from the perilous deep.

MIGNON.

Mignon is one of the most beautiful characters in Goethe's works. In her early childhood she had been carried away from her home in Italy. Wilhelm Meister, seeing her abused, became her protector. One day she sang a sweet song of her native land, and after finishing she stood silent a moment, then looking keenly at Meister, she said, "Knowest thou that land?" "It must be Italy," said Meister. "Italy?" said Mignon, with an earnest air, "If thou goest there, take me with thee." "Hast thou been there already?" said Meister. But the child was silent; nothing more could be got out of her.

KNOWEST thou the land where citron orchards bloom,
And golden oranges hang 'midst green leaves' gloom?
There gentle breezes 'neath the azure sky,
O'er silent myrtles waft the branches high;
    Say, dost thou know it? Thither, O thither,
    Might I with thee, O my beloved one, flee!

Knowest thou the house? Its walls on pillars rest,
Bright are its halls, its rooms in glittering drest,
There marble statues stand and seem to me,
To ask, "Poor child, what have they done to thee?"
    Say, dost thou know it? Thither, O thither,
    Might I with thee, O my protector, flee!

11

Kennst du den Berg und seinen Wolkensteg?
Das Maulthier sucht ins Nebel seinen Weg,
In Höhlen wohnt der Drachen alte Brut:
Es stürtzt der Fels und über ihn die Fluth.
Kennst du es wohl?
Dahin! Dahin!
Geht unser Weg! O Vater lass uns ziehn!

DAS SCHLOSS BONCOURT.

(EIN LEID VON CHAMISSO).

Ich traum' als kind mich zurücke,
    Und schüttle mein greises Haupt;
Wie sucht ihr mich heim ihr Bildet,
    Die lang ich vergessen geglaubt?

Hoch ragt aus schatt'gen Gehegen,
    Ein schimmerndes Schloss hervor,
Ich kenne die Thürme, die Zinnen,
    Die steinerne Brücke, das Thor.

Es schauen vom Wappenschild,
    Die Löwen so traulich mich an,
Ich grüsse die alten Bekanten
    Und eile den Burghof hinan.

Knowest thou those crags with heavy cloud-capped load,
Amidst the fogs the pack-mule seeks his road;
In caverns dwell the dragon's ancient brood,
O'er fallen rocks dashes the angry flood.
  It dost thou know indeed? Thither, O thither,
  We'll take our way, O father, let us flee!

THE CASTLE OF BONCOURT.

(TRANSLATED FROM CHAMISSO).

The Chateau de Boncourt in Champagne, was the old family residence of Chamisso's ancestors, where he was born in 1781. When the French Revolution broke out, the castle was assailed and razed to the ground, and the impoverished family, which ranked among the first of France, was obliged to flee. Chamisso was brought to Germany at the age of nine, where he spent the greater part of his life, and attained to considerable eminence as a poet. No one acquainted with the history of its author can read this poem without being touched by the sweetness and beauty of its sentiments.

I DREAM myself back into childhood,
  And shake my old grey head;
How ye suddenly seek me, ye visions,
  That I long thought forgotten and dead.

Out rises from 'midst shady gardens,
  A glittering castle so great,
I know well its battlements, towers,
  The stream, the bridge and the gate.

The lions rude-carved at the portal,
  Majestically gaze in my face;
I greet the old friends of my boyhood,
  And speed the court-yard space.

Dort liegt die Sphinx am Brunen,
   Dort grünt der Feigenbaum,
Dort hinter diesen Fenstern
   Verträumt ich den ersten Traum.

Ich tret' in die Burgkapelle,
   Und suche des Ahnhern Grab,
Dort ist's, dort hängt vom Pfeiler,
   Das alte Gewaffen herab.

Noch lesen umflort die Augen,
   Die Züge der Inschrift nicht;
Wie hell durch die bunten Scheiben,
   Das Licht darüber auch bricht.

So stehst du, O Schloss meiner Väter,
   Mir treu und fest in dem Sinn,
Und bist von der Erde verschwunden,
   Der Pflug geht über dich hin.

Sei fruchtbar O theurer Boden,
   Ich segne dich mild und gerührt,
Und segn' ihn zwiefach wer immer,
   Den Pflug nun über dich fükrt.

Ich aber will auf mich raffen,
   Mein Saitenspiel in der Hand,
Die Weiten der Erde durchschweifen,
   Und singen von Land zu Land.

There lies the Sphinx at the fountain,
    There grows the fig-tree green;
Just there behind those windows
    Dreamed I my boyhood's first dream.

I walk in the aisles of the chapel,
    And search for my ancestors' graves;
There they are, and there from the pillars
    Hang down the old armor and glaives.

Though brilliant through painted windows,
    Rainbow-like gleams the sun's light,
Still I can not read the inscription
    For tears have enveloped my sight.

Thus thou standest, O castle, my fathers,
    So faithful and fast in my mind
Though long from the earth thou art vanished,
    The plough leaves no vestige behind.

Be fruitful, dear birth-place, I bless thee,
    Though anguish o'ershadows my brow,
And doubly I bless him whoever
    Guides over thy bosom the plow.

But I will rouse me and journey,
    Like a minstrel with lyre in my hand—
Through the wide, wide world will I wander,
    Still singing from land to land.

THE INDIAN'S REVENGE.

A WILD Indian who in savage freedom
Liv'd, nor knew the white-man's art or polish —
Free of guile or cunning was his bosom,
Heart as pure as God to him had given —
Brought the game that he with bow and sinew
Far in northern unfrequented forests,
In the chase had captured, to the market;
There, without the arts of cunning trader,
He the game of mount and moorland bartered,
Taking, trusting what the white-man offered.
Joyful, proudly, with his hard-won treasures,
Hied he home to his wild forest comrades,
To his children and brown-featured consort.

But while distant from his lowly wigwam,
Suddenly a storm of bleak November
Overtook him; poured the clouds of heaven,
On his lengthened locks of raven blackness,
And the coarse and untanned deer-skin garments,
Clung to his lean form dark-skinned and sinewy.
Weary, shivering in the chilly rain-storm,
Sped with hasty step the honest savage,
Towards a house which he in distance noticed:
" Sir, permit me till the storm is over
Rest and warm me in your friendly shelter."
Thus addressing the proud pale-faced owner,
" Get thee hence, thou misshaped, dreaded savage,
Nor return thou; let me see thee never."
Thus the planter roughly spoke in anger,
Seized a knotty staff to fright the Indian.

Sad the Indian as he went reflective
Brooding o'er the white man's cruel treatment,

On through rain and gusts, till late at evening,
Came he to his rude, but peaceful, wigwam,
And to his own brown-skinned consort's welcome:
Wet and weary couched he by the fireside,
With his little, dusky offspring 'round him.
Then he told them tales of crowded cities,
Engines, cannon belching forth their thunder,
Of the wind and rain-storm that o'ertook him,
And the white man's harsh and cruel treatment;
Lovingly they bathed his brow with kisses,
Clinging to him with child-like caresses,
Sought to dry his hair, long, black and dripping;
Eagerly their father's pouch they fumbled,
Till at last they found the gifts he promised.

Months elapsed, and then the white man hunting
In the woods, he lost his path and wandered —
Over brakes and rocks, thro' streams and valleys,
Many steep cliffs climbed with footsteps weary,
Striving still to find again the pathway,
That from out this wilderness would bring him..
Vain his wanderings, vainer still his calling,
Naught received he but the hollow echo
Rolling through the cañon's rocky ridges;
Anxiously he toiled in doubt and darkness,.
Till at length, at foot of nearest mountain,
Saw a little, feeble camp-fire flickering;
Fright and joy throbbed in his breast alternate,.
Taking courage he approached with caution.
"Who comes there?," with fierce and warlike accents
Cried a voice, deep in the mountain cavern,
And a warrior stood erect before him;
"Friend, in forest long have I been wandering,"
Cried with trembling voice the frightened white man,
"Let me rest here, this night, for I'm weary,
Guide me homeward early in the morning,
And to thee will I be grateful ever."

"Come in, welcome," answered the unknown one,
"Warm thyself, for still the fire is burning."
Strode the savage to a gloomy corner,
Brought forth food as he himself had eaten —
Parched corn, wild nuts, ham of bear or venison,
To appease the wandering white man's hunger,
Who with appetite of hunter feasted,
As though at a brother's festive table;
Quietly yet gravely sat the red man
Near his guest, and watched the white man's features,
Who with hungry teeth the food divided,
And with rapture quaffed the fountain's treasure,
From a barken vessel rudely fashioned.
Then on couch of yielding moss and rushes,
Bear-skin covered, slept the pale-faced hunter,
Safely slumbered till the morning sunshine.

Like the desert-Arabs wildest war-chief,
Fearful then with knife and bow and quiver,
Stood the Indian by his guest fast slumbering,
Woke him, and the frightened white man starting,
Quickly reached to grasp his trusty weapons;
But a dish to him the Indian proffered,
Brimming over with a food nutritious;
Thus he smiling the white hunter nourished.
Then he brought him far through many windings,
Over brakes and rocks, through brooks and valleys,
Ways untrodden till they reached the highway.
Bowed with thanks to him the pale-faced hunter,
But the savage stood and darkly frowning,
Gazed with eagle eye upon the stranger,
Spoke with voice both full and firm and earnest,
" Haply ere this we have met each other?"

As by palsy stricken stood the hunter,
In his host and guide now recognizing

But the savage, calmly smiling, answered—
"Tell your prudent, wise and crafty people
That we savages have more of feeling:"
Thus he spake and vanished in the forest.

Whom he in the storm-wind forth had driven,
Dashed, confused, he stammered forth excuses,
But the savage, calmly smiling, answered—
"Tell your prudent, wise and crafty people
That we savages have more of feeling;"
Thus he spake and vanished in the forest.

OTHER POEMS.

WYNONA.

Lake Pepin is a widening of the Mississippi River. It is about twenty miles in length and from two to six miles in breadth. Near the south end of the lake is a high bluff called Maiden's Rock, the top of which seems to hang over towards the water. The Indians pretend to fix a date to the incidents narrated in this legend. They say it occurred about one hundred and fifty snows ago. They are offended if you suggest the possibility of its being a fiction. I wish I could throw into the story the feeling and energy of the Indians who related it to me while teaching school among them.

In the bright west where fades the lingering light,
Whence the last beams of sunset take their flight,
Where lawns extend that scorn Arcadian pride,
And fairer streams than famed Hydaspes glide;
Ere the bright waters of this western world
Were ever by a bark or vessel curled,
Saving the ripple of the light canoe;
Above there floated the ethereal blue,
There stood in beauty the unchanging hills,
And grassy meadows fed by numerous rills,
Were all the Indians—he alone could tell
The worth and beauty of each lovely dell.
And ere the pale-face wandered here, he dwelt
In savage freedom, many a joy he felt;
Here home returning with a steadier pace,
From bloody war-path or from glorious chase,
He laid him down and basked him in the sun,
Or told in glowing terms what he had done,
Mayhap returning with a captured deer,
His swarthy children gave a thrilling cheer,

Though dark, untutored, he had still an eye
For Nature's beauties, and could there descry,
On Nature's page, a trace of that great cause
Who made and rules the universe by laws;
Could gaze in twilight on the glowing west,
And vividly describe a land of rest,
Where fruits autumnal, flowers perennial grow,
And hushed forever every wail of woe.

Amidst the records of those days past long,
None seem more tragic or more fit for song
Than those connected with those rocks and hills,
Those far-spread prairies, or those murmuring rills;
Land of wild beauty, land of light and shade,
Here dwelt Wynona, the fair Indian maid,
And youth and spring-time threw their golden ray,
Of gay romance o'er every changing day,
Nor dwelt she there alone, for there was one,
The subject of her day-dreams, was he gone?
Life's fairest beauties seemed as shadows dim,
For her young life's best hopes were linked with him.
Chaska, the warrior, whose dark eyes shone bright,
Like northern stars in vault of wintry night,
From him Wynona soon was doomed to part,
Through love's warm eddies circled round her heart,
As the bright rays of sunset take their flight,
Leaving the scene in chilliness and night;
So disappointment spread his gloomy form,
And the clouds lowered in the gathering storm
O'er her young life. And is life what it seems?
Death chose the object of her fondest dreams,
For they who never yet o'er loved ones wept,
Whose brightest hopes have never yet been swept,
Like the pure white cloud from the summer sky,
Like rose leaves scattered by tempest high,
They cannot tell of the dark, dark night,
That settles and lowers at the heart's first blight.

Wynona, pensive, viewed his bow and spear,
And the huge antlers of the captured deer,
Which he had killed; and e'en the knife,
Which he had used in robbing them of life,
Seemed to recall wild scenes and happy hours,
And then adown her dark cheeks rolled like showers,
The burning tears. Yet she in dreams oft saw,
A brighter scene than mortal pen can draw,
A fair Elysian in far western isles,
Where skies are bright and spring eternal smiles.
But more than this, she saw her Chaska there,
Dwelling securely in that realm so fair.
And sweet to her seemed his wild warrior-song—
He seemed to wonder that she tarried long .
In this cold region, while he happy dwelt,
In that bright, western country, and ne'er felt
The pain, and anguish, and the toil, and strife,
And all the sorrows incident to life,
That here are felt in this strange world of ours;
And asked her why not stay in those bright bowers,
And range with him the hills, the vales, the plain,
Where flowers of spring, and fruits of autumn reign,
Where youth and beauty ne'er shall know decay,
Where life and light and love ne'er pass away.
He also told her of the hunting ground,
Where deer and antelope through valleys bound,
And how, when willing, they could sail away,
Like summer clouds and he, as swift as they.
And oft at evening's hour, when Sol was setting,
She'd spend an hour, half musing, half regretting,
Yet scarce could wish that he was back again,
From that bright region to this world of pain,
But rather wished life's fitful fever over,
That she might meet again her Indian lover.

Harka, the messenger, whose words brought blight
To fair Wynona's prospects, took delight

In frequent boastings of his good success,
And hoped to win her by his fair address;
For to her parents he had told his passion,
And bargained for her in the Indian fashion,
And they consented, too; we need not wonder,
For he was reckoned the best Indian hunter
Of all the chief's sons, or in any station,
In all the ton-wans * of Dacotah's nation.
What though he proffered gifts — 'twas little use:
Can gifts make lovely what we never choose?
Though parents urged, she could not feel delight
Nor comfort in his words. 'Twas sorrow's night;
Sweet Hope was hidden by the howling storm,
As when the Thunder-bird † reveals his form,
The gloomy plumage of his raven crest,
And the forked lightning issuing from his breast.
Wynona found, as all the world will prove,
That heart scarce human that does never love;
Falsehoods most base, may wrong the good and pure,
And youth may linger where temptations lure,
May list too long to love's sweet flatteries —
Linger too long where passions torrents rise.

Where the bold bluffs of Mississippi stand,
By grand old forests crowned on either hand,
Northward, the lake of Pepin rolls its waves;
Or moved by summer south-wind, gently laves
Its heaving bosom on the rocky shore,
Then with a sigh its ripples break and are no more.
'Twas yellow autumn, seven moons had been
Since first the woodland bowers were clothed in green,
Since first the spring birds woke their joyous note;
But now the north-wind ofttimes roughly smote,
And with a sad, and melancholy sound,
Swept thro' the groves and o'er the withered ground,

* Villages.
† The Dacotahs believe storms are caused by a huge bird flying through the air.

And the leaves, too, that looked so dark and green
Had changed their color to a sombre sheen;
Bitten by frosts, they fell as falls the hart,
Or wounded songster smitten by the dart.

Wynona had a foe; Harpstenah's smile
Seemed Chaska's changeful nature to beguile —
Seemed like a dark cloud in the horizon
Destined to shadow the bright, morning sun;
Harka had promised, would he now betray,
With falsehood cloud Wynona's life-long day,
O'er her fair future throw the slanderer's pall,
And with life's bitter wormwood mingle gall,
Whose harshest tone was Indian maiden's song,
Whose greatest error that she loved too long?
'Twas so; that picture fair had met the gaze
Of sullen envy, 'tis from her we trace
Many the sorrows and the ills of life,
Many the scene of tumult and of strife;
Wynona felt ingratitude's cold blast,
Scorn's biting frost, and hate's fierce hail fall fast.
Ah! yes, the heart can suffer, but not all —
Too strongly mixed the wormwood and the gall.
The heart strings wither and the spirit dies —
Dies for an object which but few can prize,
A shrine to worship, an ideal to love,
A sacred circle where the heart may move,
Nor feel that its deep secrets are unrolled —
To the stern gaze of an unfeeling world.

A group of Indian girls sat on the ground,
Harpstenah's merry laughing echoed round
The circle, and their joyous hearts respond,
As they by turns in glowing terms tell of
Scenes of wild romance and of Indian love,
Enamored lovers and of maidens fond,
The mysterious legend and the magic wand;

And there continued till the shades of night
Spread o'er the landscape, and the moon's pale light
Looked down serenely on that youthful group,
Full of high promise and of ardent hope.
In five days more the warriors would depart
For a wild buffalo chase. But, ere they start,
The dance of Ha-o-kah must be performed,
That to their teepees they return unharmed;
That they may prosper in the unequal war
And bring back trophies or the glorious scar.

'Tis eventide, the pale moon rises clear
O'er the cold waters, and the prairies wear
A silvery brightness; as the sun's bright beams
Fade in the distant horizon; or the fond dreams
Of childhood fade. Thoughts of the past,
And the bright dreams of future doomed to blast,
Crowd on hope's vision; for they little think
That they are walking near the tottering brink
Of ruined hopes, of dark dismay and shame.
Is there a purer bliss we mortals claim
Than a slow walk, in the calm vesper time,
O'er the wide prairies, listening to the chime
Of lovely cascade? Thus did Nature's child,
The young Wynona, roam, hearing the wild
Yet soothing cadence of the legend song
That Harka's voice, with its wild freedom, sung.
Thus Harka wooed, while sunset's lingering ray
Threw its soft radience o'er expiring day,
Telling her fondly that her soft dark eyes
Were lovelier far than autumn's brightest dyes;
That sweet her voice, like song of nightingale,
Or when 'twas saddened as the lone dove's wail
For its lost mate; "Doth not the dark deep stream,"
Continued he, "sparkling in morning's beam,
Reflect your form, and tell that you are fair
As the pure prairie flowers in April air?"

12

Thus did she listen to his words the while
Wondering that she had ever feared that guile
Dwelt in that breast. The lovely stars shone bright
In the deep vault of heaven; and the light
Of the pale, waning moon, so clear and cold,
Shone on the ripples as they gently rolled —
For chill November winds swept o'er the lake,
Wafting each wave till it would gently break,
With soft, sweet murmur on the pebbly shore.
Thus spent Wynona that bright eve, for o'er
The saddened future was a curtain thrown,
Nor were the events of the next day known,
Save to the eye of Him who views the heart,
Knows all its sorrows, even its keenest smart.

The morning came but not with sunshine gay —
Dark autumn clouds had hid the sky with gray;
Those dread precursors of an autumn storm
Scud swiftly onward in their gloomy form.
Early in morn the treacherous Harka went
From his own teepee to Harpstenah's tent,
Declared his love with fervent, earnest vow;
Harpstenah answered she was happy now.

Then Harka told her, that her cheery voice
Would influence even the stoic warrior's choice;
Was music sweeter than the wild bird's tone,
Said that his teepee without her was lone.
Harpstenah listened, now at length she laid
Her small hand on his arm, and thus she said:
"I hear your words, now prove that they are true —
As you will love me, so will I love you;
But there's Wynona, you have vowed to her,
While she repaid you with the bitter sneer.
Remember her, who, changeful as the wave,
Coldly refused and scorned a warrior brave.

Wert thou not shamed when on her lip the scorn,
The cold and withering scorn, was proudly worn?
Dost thou not know ere sunset gilds the west
Dacotah maidens keep the Virgin's Feast?
That Feast for virgins only is prepared,
Nor should it be by any others shared;
Then why not tell her that she is not pure!
Dost thou not know that she would fain endure
Death before that?"   And was it really so?
Nay, she was pure as the untrodden snow.

The tempter's words sound sweetly in his ear,
Revenge and hatred in his heart appear;
The Feast prepares, the maidens now advance
To join in concert in the sacred dance.
The warriors come, and Harka with the rest,
Hatred and jealousy within his breast,
Stalking toward the ring, he calls aloud,
While hushed to stillness is the murmuring crowd:
"Take hence Wynona; shall she be a guest?
She is unworthy of the Virgin's Feast!"

The pale, unhappy girl with glaring eyes
Gazes upon him, but no word replies,
Bows down her head, departs with many a frown —
As night comes on when the bright sun goes down.
To whom shall she now turn, whom ask for aid,
Where wander now, forsaken and dismayed?
Unto her brother shall she now advance?
His dark deep eye reveals the angry glance,
Yet feeling still a woman's spirit strong,
A quenchless hope that lifts from mortal wrong,
Death has no terrors, life no charms for her;
No wonder then that she should death prefer,
Throw off the mortal coil that bound her here,
And soar in freedom to a brighter sphere.

Her firm, her last resolve is quickly made,
And she in bridal robes is soon arrayed.

Across the river frowned a rock-cliff bold,
Like to a castellated tower of old;
Four hundred feet it rises from the shore —
Its perpendicular height ten scores or more;
Around its dark base breaks Lake Pepin's surge,
And on its summit sounds the maiden's dirge;
Upward she clambered o'er the rugged rocks —
The autumn wind with fitful moaning mocks —
Careless and unconcerned she stands alone,
Hope of a better life propels her on.
Wildly she casts her raven locks behind,
Her long dark tresses streaming in the wind,
Nor from those dark eyes are there angry flashes,
Nor does a tear drop steal between the lashes.
She calmly speaks of a bright western shore
Where sorrow, death and envy are no more.

"Last night," said she, "in sleep I viewed the moon,
Sat on the beach and saw her light go down,
And then the spirit of the waters rose
Calmly, and silent as the current flows.
'Wynona,' said the spirit, her voice did fill
The valley wide, and the cold waves were still,
That I might hear. And then she told of death,
And of a country where no winter's breath
Chills the bright waters. 'Fair indeed, are the
Dacotah lands, but fairer far,' said she,
'Are those bright islands in the western seas,
For green forever are the forest trees —
To that fair land,' said she, 'thou soon shalt go,
Father of waters onward still may flow,
But lovelier plains and hills and streams thou'lt view,
In that fair clime where every heart is true.'

Swiftly they urge their way, but 'tis too late,
She having finished gives herself to fate—
Smiles at each beckon, scorns the arms they reach,
Then headlong plunges to the rocky beach.

And now I leave you; I have done no wrong,
Save that I've trusted and have hoped too long."
The warriors hear her, for her voice so clear
Resounds far down the vale; and pale with fear,
The warriors listen to the mournful dirge,
Then rush to snatch her from the fatal verge,
Swiftly they urge their way, but 'tis too late,
She having finished gives herself to fate —
Smiles at each beckon, scorns the arms they reach,
Then headlong plunges to the rocky beach.

That scene is closed, that young yet throbbing breast,
With all its pangs and passions is at rest.
Shall we condemn her? she who never knew
That God hath said, no murder shalt thou do?
Unknown to her the power of faith and prayer,
She sought a rest where kindred spirits are.
Proud and majestic frown those dark, gray steeps,
And often, still, the Indian maiden weeps,
As silently she floats those rocks between,
In her frail bark; for sacred is the green ·
Where fell Wynona; and the very spot
Is pointed out, where closed her earthly lot;
Spirits, they think, are hovering near the scene,
And superstition throws a sombre sheen,
On every object as the moon's pale wake,
Throws a sweet mystery o'er the sleeping lake.
Here the Dacotah checks his wild voice shrill,
And calmly pointing to that towering hill,
Fancies he views her on the summit there,
As she her arms throws wildly in the air —
Sees her dark tresses floating unconfined,
And hears her wild dirge in the passing wind.

MINNEHAHA, November 9, 1861.

HERO AND LEANDER.

A LEGEND OF ANCIENT TIMES.

Leander was a youth of Abydos, a town on the Asiatic side of the Bosphorous.
On the opposite European shore, in the town of Sestos, lived the maiden Hero, a
priestess of Venus. Leander loved her and used frequently to swim the strait to
enjoy her company. In dark nights she held a torch to direct him; but one night a
tempest arose, his strength failed, and he was drowned. The waves bore his body
to the European shore, which, when Hero saw, she in her despair cast herself into
the sea and perished.

SEE ye there the old steeps gray?
Castle-like they each survey,
    There the golden sunshine dwells,
There the Hellespontus sweeps
Impetuous through the rocky steeps
    Of the rock-bound Dardanelles;
See ye not the breakers rear,
    Dashing on the rocky shore?
Asia they from Europe tear,
    Yet love braved their angry roar.

Moved by Cupid's venomed arrow,
Leander, Hero, feel love's sorrow —
    Doomed to Cupid's god-like power;
Boldly o'er the mountains wild,
Hunter keen, Leander toiled;
    Hero bloomed earth's fairest flower,
But the hearts of this fond pair
    By their cruel sires were wrung,
And the ambrosial fruits of love
    As aye, o'er awful perils hung.

On the crags of ancient Sestos,
Where with wave's eternal echoes
    Dash the Hellespontine swells,

The maiden sits; with loving gaze,
Abydos' distant shore surveys,
    Where her loved Leander dwells.
Sestos' and Abydos' strand
    By no bridge's arch is bound —
No bark sails from that wild shore;
    Lover's art a passage found.

O'er that dark and billowy way,
Love's torch lights him with its ray —
    Guides Leander, hopeful, brave,
When the dying daylight's glimmer
Fades in west; then springs the swimmer
    In the 'Pontus' gloomy wave,
Stems the wave with vigorous arm,
    Aiming for the distant strand,
Where on high illumined cliff,
    Waves love's torch's flaming brand.

Then, by love's contentment blest,
For a time the lovers rest,
    From the dangers of the wave;
Hero then his brow will press
With that fervent holy kiss,
    Such as love e'er gives the brave,
Till the dawning of the morn
    Rouse them from delightsome dream —
Drive him from their dear retreat
    Back to ocean's chilly stream.

Spring and summer onward march
Successively through heaven's arch,
    But these happy ones ne'er saw
Autumn's changing verdure fall;
And from icy polar hall
    Earth her wintry mantle draw.

Joyfully they saw the days
    Ever short and shorter grow —
Thanks for lengthened nights of joy
    Ever fondly they bestow.

Hero viewed the lovely ocean
Then she spake with sweet emotion,
    "Neptune, ruler of the sea,
Lovely god, can'st thou deceive?
No! the wretch I'll ne'er believe;
    Thou wert ever true to me —
, Oft may mankind prove untrue;
    Cruel is a father's heart,
Ever kind and gentle thou;
    Hast thou felt the lover's smart?

"On this barren, storm-beat rock,
I would ever lonely walk,
    And in endless sorrow pine,
But thou bring'st upon thy wave
Without boat or bridge, the brave
    To my arms, across the brine.
Full of horrors are thy depths,
    Terrible thy billowy flood,
But when love implores thy grace,
    Leander's courage thee subdued."

*   *   *   *   *

Night has come, the billows grow
Dreary, dark; her torch's glow
    Holds she as a beacon ray,
Hoping that 'midst clouds and wind
He shall see the beacon kind,
    She had placed to light the way,
Cheery as the evening star.

O'er that dark and billowy way,
Love's torch lights him with its ray.

Dark the sea; the storm gusts whirl,
Deepest midnight shades unfurl;
    Stars and moon extinguished are.

Night, her mantle stretches far,
Furious the torrents pour
    From the cavernous gloomy clouds,
Lightnings flash amidst the gloom,
Loud is heard the thunder boom,
    And the monster tempest crowds
Down this dark tempestuous gulf.
    Mighty chasms foam and hiss,
Billows rise like mountains high,
    Then they sink to vast abyss.

Hero now to Neptune bows,
Fervently repeats her vows,
    Proffers all that she can give
To the storm-god grim, severe —
Sacrifices rich and dear,
    If Leander only live.
Angry, he refuses all;
    Winds extinguish torch, no trace
Guides the swimmer, dark the pall,
    Brooding o'er the landing place.

Faithless Hellespont's still form
Was the lull before the storm;
    Thou wast like a mirror bright,
Then the lover thee believed,
By thy falseness was deceived,
    In the midst the stormy night
Threw its veil across his path;
    Vain he stems the midway stream,
Storms upon him wreak their wrath,
    O'er him Furies madly scream.

Ah! the perils of the deep,
Ventured more as oft escaped.
  'Twas the mighty god's decree —
At love's parting plighted troth,
Holy love had bound them both.
    Naught but death could set him free.
In the midnight's darkest hour,
  'Round him rages tempest wild,
Now Leander feels their power,
    Though he's ocean's favored child.

*   *   *   *

Now the wild winds all are still,
Clear upon the eastern hill
  Sun's swift. horses mount and flee.
Peaceful through the vale below,
Hellespont now calm can flow,
  Smiling both the land and sea,
Gently now the ripples lave
  Softly on the rocky shore,
Glittering, playing thus the wave
  Wafts a corpse upon the shore.

Yes, 'tis he, but life is gone,
Holy kept the vow he'd given,
  Quickest glance, she knows 'tis he,
Still is heard no murmuring sound,
Not a tear-drop meets the ground,
  Calm, she gazes on the sea,
Fixed upon the waves her glance,
  Courage lights a sacred glow
Fairer than the evening tints,
  Noble as an angel's brow.

Clad in priestess flowing white,
Plunged she from the rocky height,
   In the dark and chilly wave;
Then the sea-weed was her pillow,
And the ever-rolling billow
   Was the holy corpse's grave:
'Pontus content with his spoil,
   Joyfully now rolls, and throws,
From his unexhausted fount,
   That sweeping flood that ever flows.

HOPE.

HOPE! thou art man's surest friend, and
They who cling to thee will find the
Ills of life like clouds upon a
Summer sky, which quickly pass, and
Leave the heavens clear.

                 One lesson
I have learned in life, whate'er my
Fate, to be content and wait; no
Night so long but day did come; no
Storm so wild but rested in a
Calm. Each day is fraught with lessons
Of true philosophy that pass
Unheeded by, which, turned to good
Account, would lessen sorrow, smooth
The rugged path of life. But how
Frail is man! how feeble, too; like
The caged bird he frets away a
Few brief years, then, sullen, sinks
Into the grave: that mighty

Leveler of mortal grandeur.
Where the worm alike revels on
The proud and the inglorious
Clay; impanneled in death's dark vault,
Distinctions cease, and chaos leaves
No trace of him who sat upon
A throne, or him who, clothed in
Garments vile, begged the poor pittance
Of his daily bread. Poor, toilworn
Man, racked with cares innumerable,
Yet oft imaginary; struggling
With contending passions; battling
'Gainst an unknown fate, with weapons
All unseen, hurrying thee on to
Certain death —is this thy end?

                         And
After all, what is life? Each day
Is a page of promise, the whole
A volumn of disappointments;
And yet, if rightly understood,
'Tis a pleasing narrative; a
Lesson for eternity; a
Prelude to that mighty unknown
World beyond. And the grave is heaven's
Vestibule, from whence, clothed in
Perfection's garb, the soul rises
To mingle with immortal things.
This is life's sweetest hope, with which
No man is poor, and he who has
It not, is like the helmless bark
Upon the ocean — the sport of
Every fickle wave — his soul is
Bankrupt, for he is poor, is poor
Indeed who has no hope, and sees
No light or life beyond the grave.

JUDAS.

In Time's most memorable tragedy,
Judas, a prominent figure, ever stands;
While earth shall roll he cannot be forgot.
What was his sin? Was he a traitor vile,
Or did he wish to aggrandize his Lord,
And herald in Messiah's peaceful reign?
Let us review the facts of Holy Writ,
Nor stigmatize because it is the rule.

'Tis said of Judas, he was frank and bold —
Almost to rashness bold, yet sensitive;
Who took his dreams for firm realities;
Who, once believing, all in all believed;
Rushing at obstacles and scorning risk,
Ready to venture all to gain his end.
No compromise or subterfuge for him —
His thoughts went from his brain straight to the act:
Yet with this ardent and impatient mood,
Was joined a visionary mind, that took
Impressions quick and fine, yet deep as life.
Therefore it was that in this subtle soil,
The Master's words took root, and grew, and flowered.
He heard and followed and obeyed; his faith
Was serious, earnest, real — of the crowd,
Judas, it seems, believed he was the Lord,
The true Messiah of the Jews: would he
Betray his Master for a bribe? He who
Was brave when all the rest had fled away?
Brave to return 'midst foes the paltry bribe,
Confess his sin, declare Christ's innocence!

He doubted not like some who walked with him,
· Desired no first place, as did James and John,

43

Denied Him not with Peter, not to him,
His Master said, "Away! thou'rt an offence;
Get thee behind me Satan,"—"Am I
So long time with ye and ye know me not?"
Calm, unambitious, nor moved by desire
To gain a post of honor when his Lord
Should come to rule; chosen from out the midst
Of scores of men as his apostle,— then
Again selected to a place of trust—
Unselfish, honest, he among them walked,
Haply translators since have dubbed him thief.
Why call him villain who for greed of gain
For thirty silver pieces sold his Lord?
Does not the bribe seem all too small and mean?
He held the common purse, and had he wished,
Had daily power to steal and lay aside
A secret and accumulating fund,
And had he done so he risked naught of fame;
In life he braved the scorn of all the world.

Meek followers of the lowly Nazarene—
Who, Lord of all, had not a place to rest;
Besides, why chose they for their almoner
A man so lost to shame, so foul with greed,
Or why, if he was known to be so vile,
(And who can hide his baseness at all times)
Keep him in high position to the last?
Naught, naught in all his life, by acts or words,
Shows the consummate villain that full grown
Leaps all at once to such a depth of crime.
Firm in the faith that Jesus was the Lord—
The great Messiah, sent to save the world,—
He, seeking for a sign, not for himself
But to show proof to all that He was God,
Conceived this plan, rash if you will, but grand;
Thinking Him man, he said, "Mere mortal man,

They seek to seize him. I will make pretence,
To take the public bribe and point him out,
And they shall go all armed with swords and staves —
Strong with the power of law to seize on him —
And at their touch he, God Himself, shall stand
Revealed before them, and their swords shall drop,
And, prostrate all before Him, shall adore,
And cry, 'Behold the Lord and King of all.' "
But when the soldiers laid their hands on Him,
And bound Him as they would a prisoner vile,
With taunts and mockery, and threats of death —
He all the while submitting — then his dream
Burst into fragments with a crash; aghast
The whole world reeled before him; the dread truth
Swooped like a sea upon him, bearing down
His thoughts in wild confusion. He who dreamed
To ope the gates of glory to his Lord,
Opened instead the prison's jarring door,
And saw above him, his dim dream of love
Change to a Fury stained with blood and crime;
And then a madness seized him, and remorse,
With pangs of torture, drove him down to death.

Call him not traitor; would such one whose heart
Is cased to shame, fling back the paltry bribe?
And where he knew his Master was condemned,
Rush forth in horror, but to seek his death?
Was he from man's society driven out?
Did all men flee his presence, till he found
Life too intolerable? Nay, not so!
Death came too soon upon the heels of crime.
The nation claimed what he had done was just,
At least no crime. 'Twas not the upper class
Alone — the rabbis, Pharisees and priests —
The lower mob as well, all, all cried out,
"Give us Barabbas: Jesus, to the cross!"

Where Judas spent that dark, momentous night
The sacred narrative revealeth not;
What horrible revulsions must have passed,
Across that spirit in those few last hours,
What storms that tore up life even to its roots!
Say what you will—grant all the guilt—and still
What pangs of dread remorse—what agonies
Of desperate repentance—all too late,
In that wild interval between the crime
And its atonement partial; life, the while
Laden with horror all too great to bear,
And pressing madly on death's dark abyss.
Next morn, the ghastly shadow of a man
With robes all soiled and torn, and tangled beard
Into the chamber where the council sat,
Came, feebly staggering; scarce would one have known
' Twas Judas, with that haggard, blasted face;
So had that night's great horror altered him
As one who blindly walking in a dream.
He to the table came, against it leaned,
Glared wildly, quickly round, then stretching forth,
From his torn robes, a trembling hand, flung down,
As if a snake had bit him, a small purse
That broke and scattered its white coins about,
And with a shrill voice cried: "Take back the purse!
'Twas not for that foul dross I did the deed—
'Twas not for that—oh, horror! not for that!
Only that I believed he was the Lord,
And that he is the Lord I still believe;
But oh, the sin! the sin! I have betrayed
Innocent blood, and I am lost! am lost!"
So crying, round his face he drew,
And blindly rushed away and headlong fell.

＊   ＊   ＊   ＊   ＊   ＊

This was no common mind that thus could feel—
No vulgar villain sinning for reward.

CHANGE.

These sunset moments are lovely now,
They are falling soft on my weary brow —
    Weary with rueful roaming.
Yes, soft and sweet as the zephyr's sigh,
That hushes the soul with its lullaby,
    In the calm and peaceful gloaming.
There's a plaintive pleasure around me cast,
Enticing my spirit away to the past.

These tall shadows stretched on the gilded plain,
Low whisper that sunset is with us again —
    Like monitor spirits I find them.
These shadows, where are they? Ah me! they are flown,
They have followed the sun to his regions unknown,
    And have left but this moral behind them —
"We are emblems, too true, of life's prettiest things,
Even pleasures and friendships are shadows with wings."

Dear friendship! I gaze, but discover you not —
In the PAST you appear but a featureless blot,
    Where no bright ray is beaming.
Sweet Pleasure! I listen thy music no more;
Thy melody's siren allurement is o'er —
    It is changed to unhallowed dreaming.
Ah, yes, rueful Change, *thou* indeed art the pall
That dims life's sunniest green spots all.

Proud princely towers, where once the song
Of wassail mirth, from the lordly throng,
    Echoed through hall and turret!
Are tenantless — roofless — silent all —

And the rough moss grows on the crumbling wall,
    While the night-owl murmurs o'er it;
And the homage of Ruin is mutely paid
On the shrine which merciless Change has made.

Those stately thrones, and those powers that sway
The destinies of our world to-day,
    Must perish like those before them;
And others — yea, and others anew —
Shall follow to fall and perish too,
    As Change, on his mission, creeps o'er them;
For Change is the worm that dieth not,
Till he bringeth all to "the common lot."

The homestead hearth is now cold and lone —
The hearts that gladdened it — all save one —
    Wax'd faint, and droop'd, and perish'd.
And that lone one only lives and feels,
And ponders and throbs, but nought reveals
    Of the loves so fondly cherish'd.
It is lingering out its lonesome day,
And brooding, with smiles, o'er its own decay.

Oh! where are the lov'd ones? No answer returns;
No voice can be heard in those cold, clay urns,
    Where the fond and the fair lie sleeping.
The soul starts back from the dismal thought,
Nor finds the balm she so eagerly sought,
    Though she sought it even with weeping.
She shrinks from the world in mute distress,
And lives in her own sad loneliness.

YE PAST! YE PAST! will ye not return!
Must the eye still weep, and the heart still mourn
    In plaintive, broken numbers?
Is there naught in the wide — the sovereign range

Controlcd by the great magician, Change,
    That can call you from your slumbers?
No!— Memory weeps, but must weep in vain —
For, ah! ye can ne'er return again!

But Change is coming, on rainbow wings,
To brighten the earth with happier things,
    He cometh with truth for error —
With love for hate—with joy for woe,
He cometh to make the world below
    Pure Virtue's humble mirror.
Where freedom and harmony—peace and love,
Shall be shadowed forth from the world above.

PAST AND FUTURE: A NEW YEAR'S RHYME.

Again the day is come that marks as gone
Of my life's jewels yet another one;
Another year!—ay, jewels are they all,
Of little price when many seem in store;
But gaining value as their numbers fall
From few to less, instead of few to more;
Becoming priceless most, when least of all
They are of use, and mock our longing call.
With silent pointings to the wasted part —
Wasted with, ah! how much of impure art!—
Looming amongst the silent halls of time,
Dead echoes of an unforgotten chime,
And pointing thence to years to come, ah, me!
Which may be ours—but also may not be;
Or, if they be, are of that duller kind
To which the body clings without the mind.
And here I stand and wonderingly gaze

Upon this life of mine — half done or more,
Oh! for the power to recall many a phase,
To use it better than I did before!
Thus do we think, after the strife is done,
Before the lost ground has again been won;
But if this life could be lived o'er again,
Should we be better for the less of pain
Experience has taught us to incur,
Or worse for feeling not her healthy spur?
Vain is the wish, and vainer yet the thought
To have undone what ne'er can be unwrought;
Youth with the wisdom of old age, who dreams
'Twere summer heat without the sun's glad beams!
And looking back into the checquered past,
Its griefs, its pangs, I do not stand aghast;
Though grieving for lost opportunities;
Though shaming at victorious vanities;
Though penitent for much that's done amiss,
For not aye spurning the world's Judas-kiss.
For none won battles who none ever lost;
And few love virtue who know not her cost!
And therefore do I not discard the past
As dead and gone, as useless, now, at last.
It is the sum of all my present being,
The overture to all, which dimly seeing,
Regenerate, nobler, in my kind and me.
It is experience lights the hallowed fire,
By which mankind is taught to shun the mire,
Which drew us once to its deep hidden brink,
Its meteoric, poisonous sludge to drink!
Hence, be thou welcome unto me, New Year!
Though strange thy course, I greet thee without fear,
Though I do love the past, no enmity
I bear to thee, but welcome to my heart:
An opportunity for good, for truth, for art!
For what we have achieved we need not thee,
But all the balm for what's wrong lies in thee;

For who shall say the last good now is ours?
But he who doubts the everlasting powers
By which the soul is drawn towards new lights,
To ignore which means death or hidden blights.
Ah, little soul! who thinkest nothing good,
But what delights thine own poor, worn-out mood,
As if what thou now deem'st the best and last,
Had not been scorned by generations past!
There is no end to man's aspiring thought,
As long as thought with nobleness be fraught.
The end is but in Him who was the First,
Until He says: Enough! the soul will thirst!
Thirst after greater truths and truer good,
And so run on for aye, thou human flood!
'Tis not for human hands to stem the tide,
Which only shall by Sovereign will subside.

TO UNSEEN FRIENDS.

Though on earth we've had no meeting,
Still I send you words of greeting
That may stir our souls with echoes
    From that far-off seraph shore;
Ere we left the golden portals
Of the home of the immortals,
Where in our primeval childhood,
    Sported we in days of yore.

Here the sorrowing, heavy-laden,
Still by faith may see that aiden
Where the good and true the victory gained,
    Shall joy forevermore.

What though clouds and storms surround us,
Though in darkness they have bound us,
Yet we know the sun is shining
    High above the tempest roar.

Thus my heart seems sometimes swelling,
With a joy beyond all telling;
As though in my memory lingered,
    . Echoes of that golden shore —
Telling of the waves of gladness,
Ere our hearts were stung with sadness,
Ere we left our parents mansion,
    Or these mortal forms we wore.

O, my distant friends and brothers,
We are each and all another's,
And the heart that gives most freely
    From its treasure hath the more;
For in giving love we find it,
With a golden chain we bind it,
Like an amulet of safety
    To our hearts for evermore.

REQUIEM FOR GEN. GRANT.

Toll the bell mournfully, toll the bell slow,
Toll the bell solemnly, toll the bell low:
The chief of our land is taken away,
The nation in grief is mourning to-day:
Mantle his form with the flag of our land,
The symbol of peace then place in his hand

CHORUS: Toll the bell mournfully, toll the bell slow,
Toll the bell solemnly, toll the bell low;
The chieftain beloved is taken away,
The nation in grief is mourning to-day.

Toll the bell mournfully, toll the bell slow,
Toll the bell solemnly, toll the bell low.
Thousands of veterans grieve o'er his tomb,
Millions of freemen mourn in their home;
Foemen no longer feel hate in their breast,
But weep as they lay the old soldier to rest.

Toll the bell mournfully, toll the bell slow,
Toll the bell solemnly, toll the bell low:
Think of his toil when the nation was sad,
Think of his kindness when peace made us glad;
Fierce to the foeman in battle's rude blast,
Kind to that foe when the struggle was past.

Toll the bell mournfully, toll the bell slow,
Toll the bell solemnly, toll the bell low;
High on his tomb the banner unfold,
Sculpture his name in letters of gold;
Think of his deeds as we lay him to rest,
Where naught shall disturb the peace of his breast.

Toll the bell mournfully, toll the bell slow,
Toll the bell solemnly, toll the bell low,
One more great shrine in our great and free land;
One more great name in fame's temple shall stand;
One more great page in history is wrought—
For men of all ages a lesson's been taught.

UNKNOWN HEROES.

OH, will no one sing the heroes,
  Heaped in thousands slain,
As they in glory fighting
  On the battle plain?
    Are they now to be forgotten
      In their crimson graves?
    Land they fought for, bled for, died for,
      Sing you not your braves?

CHORUS: Strike the saddest chords of music
      For the heroes gone;
    Sing them softly, hearts that loved them,
      In your sweetest song—
  . Sing them softly, hearts that loved them,
      In your sweetest song.

Hearths are cold and hearts are lonely
  That were warm and gay,
But the forms that made them happy
  Where are they to-day?—
    Dead beneath the turf they fought on,
      Flowers alone to tell,
    With their rank and florid beauty
      Where in death they fell.

For the great in combat fallen,
  Fame forever smiles;
Mournful dirges, swelling grandly,
  Flood the dreaming aisles;
    But for those we parted, weeping
      At our humble door,
    Sighs and tears, in gloom and silence,
      Mingle evermore.

A NOAD TO BLONDIN.

remarkabel pusson! enterprisin Stranger!
You left the Shoars ov frans, wair you youse to liv,
& landed hear, taking at 1's a Hi Stan.
You hev mutch genus & apperiently few cloaths.
Your intelegent feachers Speaks well Ballanst mind,
& we al no youv got a well Ballanst Body.
You must Be good, for we all no you wock
A strait and narer path which few kin foller.
altho thin clad your not a Shiftless pusson,
fur you Support yourself uncommon well.
Sumbody's warnd you Bout the 1st fals Step,
fer all kin see yourm cairful not to taik it.

remarkable pusson! perfick Biznis man!
wus it a gal that got you onto a string?
Exkews me ef i tech a tender cord —
i woodnt hirt your feelings for the world.
what Sercus man did you taik lessons ov?
You probbly Startid onto a rale rode trac,
or praps a curb stun; then you took to fensis;
& then you Soared to rafters of noo houses,
a Scairin al the Carpenters like mischief;
then "Roaps" was whispered By your guardian angel —
to which you listened with a Swete Sirpris,
& ordered ov a Balens poal imejitly.

remarkabel pusson! forever tremanjus,
Bi merely takin; ov a wock, you cleer
1,000 dolers neerly every time.
Besides, you walk into al pepels afackshuns.
the Hier you git the Stroiter you kin wock.
this shows you aint of al like Common foax.

Which can't wock mutch when they air elevated. .
Youm Consecraited for to wock a roap.
Ef i wus young (wich Strictly Speaking ain't troo,)
& hedent no wife, likewise no tender infans,
i thinc ide lern for to wock a roap miself.

remarkabel pusson! preservin'frenchman!
did you leve eny 1st chop men in frans?
ide bet there ain't no smarter men than you there!
Did lewis napolin ever see you wock?
Ef so, perhaps he got a Hint or 2
that learnt him for to keep the roap himself.
they Say sum pepel go to see you fall,
& cuss perfusely when they see you doant.
Fein french, ov coars you would plese your frens;
But probbly you ain't french enuf for that,
Becos it woodent pay as well as wockin;
Besides, you coodent get your life inshoored.

remarkabel pusson! Elivatid carricter!
Wot is your cam opiny ov america?
You must hev moments ov profound reflekshun
While a standin onto your Hed so dignified.
We Shood Be Sorry to Hev you go away
& say that things Heer doant egsackly Soot.
Weer very angshus for to· pleese grait foriners.
air you pleesed with niagry, mr. Blondin? praps
it ain as good, for a fall, as some in frans,
But it roars cuite passibel, sumtime in the night.·
You air admired, grait foriner, by thousands.·
Keep on a wockin, mr.· Blondin. adoo.

WORKS OF J. H. WARD.

The Hand of Providence,

Showing the Instrumentalities Used by Divine Providence for the Civilization and Amelioration of the Nations of the Earth.

PRICE, 60 CENTS.

WE most cordially express the pleasure and edification with which we have perused its contents, and would recommend it to our young people as a work vastly worthy of acceptation. It will give them a readiness in historical information, which they would be long in acquiring in the general mode of historical research. — *Deseret News.*

A BOOK deeply interesting to all classes of readers and of especial benefit to the young or those who have limited means of information. It should find a place in every library. — *Logan Journal.*

THE historical information it contains is really wonderful in so small a volume. As a book of reference it will prove a treasure, and the way in which the author demonstrates the Hand of Providence is above worth the price of the book. — *Hannah T. King.*

Gospel Philosophy,

Showing the Absurdities of Infidelity and the Harmony of the Gospel with Science and History. Illustrated with Numerous Engravings.

PRICE, 75 CENTS.

IT is an excellent, tersely-written volume, and contains a vast amount of scientific and historical information, and is illustrated with numerous engravings. — *Juvenile Instructor.*

No other work can be perused more profitably by the young; we can therefore recommend its use in every Sunday School, Improvement Association and home of the Saints. — *Deseret News.*

Ballads of Life,

Illustrated with Numerous Engravings from Original Designs by Weggeland.

PRICE, $1.25.

In preparation,

Great Cities of the World,

Their Glory, their Sins and their Desolations.

Any of the above works mailed to any address, on receipt of price, by

JOS. HYRUM PARRY & CO., SALT LAKE CITY, UTAH.

OTHER PUBLICATIONS

History and Philosophy of Marriage,

Or, Polygamy and Monogamy Compared. By a Christian Philanthropist.

PRICE, $1.

Are We of Israel?

A Research into the Israelitish Lineage of the Latter-day Saints. By Elder George Reynolds.

PRICE, 20 CENTS.

The "Mormon" Metropolis,

An Illustrated Guide to Salt Lake City and its Environs. Containing Illustrations and Descriptions of Principal Places of Interest to Tourists; also Interesting Information and Historical Data with regard to Utah and its People.

PRICE, 25 CENTS.

Items of Church History,

The Government of God, and the Gift of the Holy Ghost. Articles written by the Prophet Joseph Smith and Presedent John Taylor.

PRICE, 15 CENTS.

Remarkable Visions,

Containing the Visions of Stephen M. Farnsworth, George Washington and Newman Bulkley.

PRICE, 10 CENTS.

Parry's Literary Journal,

A Monthly Magazine of the Very Best Literature.

ONLY $1.50 PER YEAR.

Any of the above works mailed to any address, on receipt of price, by

JOS. HYRUM PARRY & CO., SALT LAKE CITY, UTAH.